A Candlelight Ecstasy Romance

DID SHE DARE?

She wanted nothing more than to reach out and run her hand across the hard muscles of his chest. Slowly his hands came down and gently pulled her to him, as if he were afraid a sudden movement would make her shy away. Once held against that hard, unyielding surface, Kay pushed away all thoughts of tomorrow or yesterday and concentrated on the lips descending to hers *now*. It was a kiss of a thousand kisses. His lips softly caressing hers again and again, breaking down her last wall of resistance like a battering ram of the finest velvet. She wanted him now and forever. Once and for all.

A CANDLELIGHT ECSTASY ROMANCE ®

122 A SILENT WONDER, *Samantha Hughes*
123 WILD RHAPSODY, *Shirley Hart*
124 AN AFFAIR TO REMEMBER, *Barbara Cameron*
125 TENDER TAMING, *Heather Graham*
126 LEGACY OF LOVE, *Tate McKenna*
127 THIS BITTERSWEET LOVE, *Barbara Andrews*
128 A GENTLE WHISPER, *Eleanor Woods*
129 LOVE ON ANY TERMS, *Nell Kincaid*
130 CONFLICT OF INTEREST, *Jayne Castle*
131 RUN BEFORE THE WIND, *Joellyn Carroll*
132 THE SILVER FOX, *Bonnie Drake*
133 WITH TIME AND TENDERNESS, *Tira Lacy*
134 PLAYING FOR KEEPS, *Lori Copeland*
135 BY PASSION BOUND, *Emma Bennett*
136 DANGEROUS EMBRACE, *Donna Kimel Vitek*
137 LOVE SONG, *Prudence Martin*
138 WHITE SAND, WILD SEA, *Diana Blayne*
139 RIVER ENCHANTMENT, *Emma Bennett*
140 PORTRAIT OF MY LOVE, *Emily Elliott*
141 LOVING EXILE, *Eleanor Woods*
142 KINDLE THE FIRES, *Tate McKenna*
143 PASSIONATE APPEAL, *Elise Randolph*
144 SURRENDER TO THE NIGHT, *Shirley Hart*
145 CACTUS ROSE, *Margaret Dobson*
146 PASSION AND ILLUSION, *Bonnie Drake*
147 LOVE'S UNVEILING, *Samantha Scott*
148 MOONLIGHT RAPTURE, *Prudence Martin*
149 WITH EVERY LOVING TOUCH, *Nell Kincaid*
150 ONE OF A KIND, *Jo Calloway*
151 PRIME TIME, *Rachel Ryan*
152 AUTUMN FIRES, *Jackie Black*
153 ON WINGS OF MAGIC, *Kay Hooper*
154 A SEASON FOR LOVE, *Heather Graham*
155 LOVING ADVERSARIES, *Eileen Bryan*
156 KISS THE TEARS AWAY, *Anne Hudson*
157 WILDFIRE, *Cathie Linz*
158 DESIRE AND CONQUER, *Diane Dunaway*
159 A FLIGHT OF SPLENDOR, *Joellyn Carroll*
160 FOOL'S PARADISE, *Linda Vail*
161 A DANGEROUS HAVEN, *Shirley Hart*

A PASSIONATE VENTURE

Julia Howard

A CANDLELIGHT ECSTASY ROMANCE ®

Published by
Dell Publishing Co., Inc.
1 Dag Hammarskjold Plaza
New York, New York 10017

Copyright © 1983 by Patricia K. Adams-Manson

All rights reserved. No part of this book may be
reproduced or transmitted in any form or by any
means, electronic or mechanical, including photocopying,
recording or by any information storage
and retrieval system, without the written permission
of the Publisher, except where permitted by law.

Dell ® TM 681510, Dell Publishing Co., Inc.

Candlelight Ecstasy Romance®, 1,203,540, is a registered
trademark of Dell Publishing Co., Inc.,
New York, New York.

ISBN: 0-440-16076-6

Printed in the United States of America
First printing—August 1983

To my Sweet William, with love

To Our Readers:

We have been delighted with your enthusiastic response to Candlelight Ecstasy Romances®, and we thank you for the interest you have shown in this exciting series.

In the upcoming months we will continue to present the distinctive sensuous love stories you have come to expect only from Ecstasy. We look forward to bringing you many more books from your favorite authors and also the very finest work from new authors of contemporary romantic fiction.

As always, we are striving to present the unique, absorbing love stories that you enjoy most—books that are more than ordinary romance.

Your suggestions and comments are always welcome. Please write to us at the address below.

Sincerely,

The Editors
Candlelight Romances
1 Dag Hammarskjold Plaza
New York, New York 10017

CHAPTER ONE

"He can't fire you—you work for me!"

Kay Pagel had been expecting such a move, but that didn't lessen her anger at Burke Huntingdon's treatment of her employees.

It had been a coup for Pagel Associates to win the contract with Southey, but now Kay wondered just how much of a victory her small training firm had actually won. They'd only been a month into the project when Southey was bought out by a large corporation in one of the smoothest takeovers she'd ever seen. And now Burke Huntingdon, as its new president, had let her two best employees go.

"Call it dismissed, then, the effect is the same," Gloria Larson replied. "Huntingdon does *not* want us around Southey Manufacturing, Kay."

"Gloria, you and Steve are Pagel Associates' best consultants. Corporate maneuvering isn't uncommon in a new takeover, so don't take Huntingdon's actions too personally," Kay said. "Why don't both of you transfer to the Wilson account? I can manage this thing with Southey; I'll go straight to Huntingdon himself."

After a relieved Gloria had gone, Kay sat thrumming her pencil against the desk pad. The eraser bounced rapidly with a staccato beat, then stopped. She flipped a switch to call her secretary.

"Mary, call Southey Manufacturing—I want to see Burke Huntingdon immediately!"

An hour later she jabbed the button for the fourth floor of Southey's San Diego corporate office building. Her chin was tilted at a determined angle as she considered the imminent meeting with Huntingdon; the quiet hum of the elevator was a perfect backdrop for her agitation. Both Southey Manufacturing and Burke Huntingdon were going to learn that, contract or no contract, she would *not* allow her employees to be treated in such a way.

Walking off the elevator, Kay had to stop short to keep from colliding with an unmoving mass that was thoroughly masculine. She deeply inhaled his musky scent before stepping back, though her confused senses were willing to stay near him.

"Pardon me," she said, glancing at the man absently. With an impatient hand she brushed back a lock of soft brown hair and was about to continue on her way when her mind registered his identity. She froze.

Standing two inches over six feet, Burke Huntingdon towered over her smaller frame. "Of course," he said, his deep resonant voice washing over her.

Her business instincts—always excellent—took over and the golden combination of her shoulder-length light-brown hair, amber eyes, and tanned skin created the daunting impression of gilt armor. Though a good seven inches shorter than the blond man in front of her, she faced him squarely.

"Mr. Huntingdon, I'm Kay Pagel; I was just on my way to our meeting." Kay looked directly into his blue eyes, challenging him to dismiss her. Her hand went out to shake his and their handclasp was solid but brief. The look that flashed through his eyes when he heard her name was neither angry nor defensive, as she had expected, but *impatient*. Her stomach stirred in uneasy warning.

With a jolt of awareness she saw three other men standing behind Huntingdon. She was startled to see how insignificant they seemed when compared to the overpowering attraction of the man in front of her. Attraction? Shaking her head to deny the word, she swept her amber eyes back over his face and caught a flicker of surprise. He'd forgotten their meeting!

Her eyes told Huntingdon nothing as they gazed levelly back at him, but she knew immediately that she had read his expression correctly. He had obviously underestimated her.

"We did have an appointment at ten thirty this morning, Mr. Huntingdon. Perhaps you forgot?"

"I was headed there right now." His voice had deepened with his irritation. He glanced at the men behind him to warn them not to contradict his statement; they remained silent.

"Indeed? I was told we were to meet in the fourth-floor conference room. The one at the end of this hallway, I believe." Her head inclined slightly to indicate the direction from which he had come. One of his dark-blond eyebrows rose at her challenge, a glint of interest flaring in his eyes.

"Ed," he said, not turning from her, "I'll meet you later in your office. Frank, John, I'll get back to you this afternoon." The three men made their way around the two combatants with politely murmured assents.

"I need to get some papers from my office," he told her after the men had gone. "If you would care to wait for me in the conference room, Miss Pagel, I'll be with you in ten minutes." The flare of interest had died and his eyes iced over completely.

"*Dr.* Pagel," she corrected. Looking pointedly at her watch to hold him to his time limit as well as to avoid the chill from his eyes, she said, "Very well, I'll meet you there in ten minutes."

The corridor was wide, but she had to brush against his arm to walk past him. The contact lasted only an instant, but it sent alarms clanging up and down her nervous system. They both jerked away from the touch, and though unsettled by her reaction, she continued down the hall.

After a moment she heard the faint whisper of the opening elevator doors and turned at the sound. Her eyes met Huntingdon's as he watched her from the elevator, an invisible bond holding them across the distance until the closing doors severed it.

Kay knew she was a good businesswoman, but Huntingdon was rumored to be tenacious, efficient, and sure of what pleased and displeased him. Could she hold her own against him? The rustle of her crisp white linen suit reassured her as she entered the conference room.

Fifteen minutes later she was looking out the window when the door to the conference room opened. Suddenly the room felt filled to capacity, although she knew that, when she turned, only one tall blond man would be there.

"I'm relieved to see you could finally visit Southey," he said, taking off his suit jacket and hanging it over a chair. "Are you here to protest about your employees' dismissal or to work?" He crossed his arms in front of him, the pull of his pale blue shirt over his muscled arms distracting her.

"I've been busy with another client. But since you've dismissed my two best employees, I've decided to handle the account myself." The words were out before she realized what she was saying.

"Evidently your other client was more important than Southey," he said, his eyes roaming over her.

Her lush figure was only hinted at beneath the severe lines of her suit, though he appeared to appreciate what he saw. She was still standing in front of the window, the light streaming through her hair and highlighting the hidden strands of spun gold, lightening it to match the color of her eyes; it was an undeniably appealing combination. The armor had melted away in the sunlight.

"No, they are merely clients of longer standing. I've reassigned to that company both of the employees you dismissed," she told him, hoping he would understand that such a move showed her trust in them.

"Do you think that was wise, Dr. Pagel? If they were unable to perform here . . ."

She fumed silently, hating to be put on the defensive. "Gloria Larson and Steve Sterling are both excellent training consultants. And that is what we are, Mr. Huntingdon, consultants, not clairvoyants."

They had remained standing, his height still putting her at a disadvantage, though more than just his towering frame disturbed her. That thought was quickly brushed away with a mental snort of derision. The idea of "chemistry" between two people was ludicrous! In her thirty-one years she'd never felt the slightest twinge beyond a vague sort of excitement that soon faded. But she couldn't deny that her body was reacting oddly to this man.

Trying to diminish his effect on her, she sat down at the table, using the slab of wood between them to guard her unusual susceptibility. Unfortunately, as he sat down opposite her, she realized too late that her maneuver had only brought them closer together. She frowned in frustration as he spoke firmly.

"Dr. Pagel, after reading your excellent article in *Training Quarterly*, I agreed with Southey's retired president to let your firm stay on and try to do what Southey's own in-house staff could not—remedy our production problems."

He went through the stack of papers he'd brought with him and pulled out a copy of her article. "But do the ideas expressed in here still hold?" The challenge in his eyes was unmistakable.

She frowned at the implied accusation. "Of course those ideas still hold. But your reasons for dismissing Larson and Sterling had nothing to do with what I said in that article. Do you even *want* Pagel Associates to continue with this project, Mr. Huntingdon? If you would rather bring in another firm . . ." She let the sentence hang in the air between them.

"It won't be that easy. We have a contract and I expect you to fulfill it."

"Then, may we get on with it?" she said, leaning forward, her elbow on the table. An answering challenge made her eyes glow with a molten fire.

Matching her posture, he leaned forward, his advantage in height bringing his face to within inches of hers. For a moment they said nothing and Kay was startled by the sheer magnetism the man exuded. "Whenever you feel up to it, Dr. Pagel," he said, breaking the silence.

Her breath caught at his blatant sarcasm and she had to sit back for a moment before continuing.

"First, I would like to tour your facilities and talk with some of your people; then I need to have each of your department heads submit a report to me regarding problems in their individual areas.

"After reading those, I'll want to do some checking on my own. I'll complete the task analysis using some of the work that's already been done. Then we can start on the design. Does that schedule meet with your approval?" Her eyes were cool as they met his in polite inquiry. But then, her eyes didn't reflect her heart's pulsing beat as it sent heated blood speeding through her veins.

Once before she'd felt this excitement at just being with a man, though she didn't remember Matt being quite this disturbing. But that had been nine years ago, when she had just started her second year of graduate school; the affair with Matt had ended before the semester.

"Fine." Huntingdon rose, his lithe frame looming over her as he bent to ask, "Are you ready? We can leave for your tour right now."

"Right now?" She was unprepared for his abrupt decision. "Don't you want to finish our discussion? I have several ideas I'd like to talk over with you." She started to retrieve her notes from her briefcase.

"Why not now? Your schedule is satisfactory; what more is there to discuss?"

Instinctively she knew she shouldn't go on the tour with him, though she had trouble putting her objections into words. Glancing at her watch, she exhaled in relief; it was almost twelve. "I'm sorry, Mr. Huntingdon, but I have a luncheon appointment. Could we reschedule the tour for Monday?" she asked, thinking she would have the entire weekend to gather her courage.

"I thought you wanted to get started on the project as quickly as possible. What about this afternoon? I'll be tied up in meetings, but John Danton can show you around. Can you make it back by two?"

His criticism of her weak-kneed behavior was echoed in his eyes as they bored into her, demanding an answer. As long as he wasn't going to be escorting her, she felt it was safe to agree. "Two will be fine," she said, gracefully rising to leave. His eyes followed her movement and a tiny flash of admiration escaped before he turned to put on his jacket.

Brushing close to him again as she walked out into the hallway, she could smell the musky aftershave he wore mixed with the indefinable tang of his maleness.

No words were spoken as they walked to the elevator, but the silence was interrupted as a distant door opened and Southey's employees crowded toward the elevators to leave for lunch. When the elevator arrived, Huntingdon and Kay were forced to the back of the car, she standing in front of him. The others looked curiously at Burke Huntingdon, then turned to the front; they were anxious to leave quickly once they reached the ground floor.

Huntingdon's hands rested lightly on Kay's upper arms to keep her from being jostled. To her unexpectedly tyrannic emotions, his touch felt welcome and natural, though Kay rarely let men get so close. It was frightening how her body's actions refused to be ruled by her head.

The ride seemed to take forever, with long stops at each

floor as a few more people tried to squeeze in. Huntingdon's hands began absently to stroke her arms in short, slow movements and his breath teased her hair, sending Kay's pulse into tumult.

She desperately wanted to move away from him, but the press of bodies prevented her. Her only possible response was to stand rigid and hope her tense posture would communicate her displeasure to him. The doors opened on the ground floor and she stepped away from him as soon as the pressure of the crowd allowed her to move. Turning to face him from a safe distance, she said, "Thank you, Mr. Huntingdon. I'll be looking forward to meeting Mr. Danton at two. Good-bye." She was almost free of him.

"Good-bye, Dr. Pagel," he said, preparing to accompany her to the parking lot.

The idea made her panic and she walked rapidly to catch up with the exiting lunchtime horde, leaving him once again to stare at her from the elevator car.

Her four-year-old Volvo's response was gratifying as she sped out of the parking lot and down the city streets to the freeway entrance, heading back to her office. When she arrived, she made straight for the phone and dialed Ric Adler to cancel their lunch date. He wasn't in his office, but she called their usual restaurant in Mission Valley and found him there.

"Ric! Sorry I can't make it for lunch—I got tied up at Southey. Can we make it for next week instead?" Talking to this nice, safe man made her sigh gratefully. She felt her self-control returning.

For the most part Ric was an undemanding escort and that was exactly the way she preferred it. She also had no doubts that Ric would agree to the postponement, and he did.

"Are you free tonight?" he continued. "The Padres are having an exhibition game; they're looking good this year."

"Not tonight, Ric," she answered, hoping her complete

disinterest in baseball didn't communicate itself to him. "But thanks."

"Sure. Well, see you next week—oh, is Wednesday okay?"

"Wednesday's fine."

"Great, see you then."

"Good-bye, Ric."

A few minutes passed as she doodled agitated designs on her desk pad. The phone rang and she hastily scribbled out what she had drawn there.

"Kay Pagel," she answered.

"Hi, Doc!" her brother's voice greeted her. "I don't want to keep you, but Davy's been nagging me to be sure and remind you about our picnic on Sunday. You haven't forgotten, have you?"

"Oh, Allen, what your son must think of my memory! He just called me yesterday afternoon." She laughed, recalling the five-year-old's disjointed invitation. "Don't worry, I haven't forgotten and I've already bought a sack of potatoes for the potato salad. How's Sally?"

"She's fine; said to tell you hi. Sure you won't bring anyone along with you? He'd be more than welcome," Allen said, his voice hopeful.

Kay hated to disappoint him, but said, "No, Allen, I don't think so. But be sure and tell Davy I haven't forgotten about his picnic, okay?"

"Sure thing, sis. Take care."

The conversation with her brother had lifted her spirits, and at two o'clock, when she entered Southey's corporate office building, she felt able to tackle the tour. She was shown to a well-appointed, but strictly functional, conference room similar to the one she'd been in before.

An equally functional secretary informed her that Mr. Huntingdon would be right with her.

"But I'm to meet Mr. Danton," Kay explained to the neatly dressed young woman.

"Perhaps Mr. Danton was busy. It was Mr. Hunting-

17

don's secretary who phoned down, ma'am," the woman answered politely.

"Well, thank you anyway," Kay said, frowning as she contemplated dealing with Burke Huntingdon again. Shortly after the secretary left, the door behind Kay opened and she turned in her seat with a hopeful smile on her face, thinking that perhaps the young woman *had* mistaken the names.

"Good afternoon," Dr. Pagel," Burke Huntingdon said as he entered the room. Sitting down next to Kay, he said nothing more, though her smile had made his eyes come alive with a speculative blue fire.

"Good afternoon, Mr. Huntingdon," she answered, her face once again a professional mask. "When will Mr. Danton arrive? I'm anxious to begin the tour."

"John won't be joining us; I've decided to escort you myself," he said. His mouth curved into a smile as he waited for her reaction.

Kay was not at all pleased to hear her fears put into words. She was sure her eyes reflected her unpleasant shock and she quickly lowered them. What was she going to do? With him in the background the job had been tolerable—but constantly looking over her shoulder? She'd never be able to concentrate on the job at hand—he was too . . . distracting.

Huntingdon saw only her composed features and nothing of her inner turmoil. She raised her eyes in time to see a smile hovering around his thin but oddly sensual lips.

As he met her eyes, his smile disappeared. "You seem upset at the notion of my escorting you. Do you object?"

Not being able to tell him *why* she'd rather not be near him made her answer more sharply than she'd intended. "No," she said tartly, "I don't object."

She frowned and turned the subject back to business. "But if Mr. Danton is unable to show me around right now, I'd be glad to reschedule the tour." Kay hoped her eagerness wasn't *too* perceptible.

"He won't be on this project anymore; he has been reassigned, much in the way Miss Larson was," he answered, his face impassive, but she was sure she saw an unusual light in his eyes. A chill went through her. "Now I'm overseeing the project myself."

This time Kay was sure she saw his eyes twinkle with a malign glee at her discomfort. Swallowing her alarm, trying to accept the arrangement with professional grace.

"May we begin, then?" she asked.

"Of course." He rose and opened the door.

"I have last month's production figures up in my office. We'll go pick them up and then drive down to the plant in National City."

"That sounds fine," she said.

They were quickly on the top floor of the fifteen-story building. Her feet sank into the plush carpeting and she noted how well it muffled the sound of their passing. He stopped outside a burl walnut door that reached to the ceiling.

A woman who appeared to be in her mid-forties was sitting at the nearby desk, elaborately coiffed and wearing an expensive, form-fitting dress on her spare frame, apparently with the notion that it enhanced her figure. The eyes, dark brown and heavy with makeup, stared out at them with the cold, impersonal hostility with which she must have greeted everyone, judging from Huntingdon's reaction.

He ignored his secretary's ill humor and introduced her to Kay. "Dr. Pagel, this is Carol Walsh, my secretary. Carol, this is Dr. Pagel, president of Pagel Associates." Kay ignored the daggers in the secretary's eyes and extended her arm for a handshake that was slackly returned.

"We'll probably be talking on the phone quite a bit, Miss Walsh," Kay said.

"As you say," Miss Walsh replied, her eyes not losing their chilly glint.

"Carol, I'll be out the rest of the afternoon," Huntingdon said as he put a hand behind Kay and indicated with the other that she was to enter his office. "Would you call and tell National City we'll be down in about an hour?"

Miss Walsh only nodded and returned to her work.

Kay preceded him into the office and stopped short. She felt rather than saw him enter behind her and shut the door. The office was a fantasy, and she followed the deep tan carpet as it flowed to the floor-to-ceiling windows, and stood watching the Lilliputian scene before her. Hundreds of ships filled the docks along the waterfront, huge Navy vessels alongside the smaller, more modest craft of commercial fishermen. And through it all, tiny, brightly colored sails of pleasure boats weaved intricate patterns on the water.

"This is glorious!" she whispered, turning to Huntingdon, who had seated himself behind his massive desk. His face wore an odd expression she was unable to interpret.

"You must get that reaction often," Kay said.

He smiled and Kay was surprised to discover how the harsh lines of his face lightened when that smile reached his eyes. With his proud nose thrusting up between his eyes, he could never be considered classically handsome, but at that moment he was the most attractive man she had ever seen.

"Actually, most people don't notice the view at all, but those who do usually comment on it because it's a valuable commodity." His eyes left her face and looked out the smoke-tinted window to the ships in San Diego Bay. "I find I work better when I can see out of doors."

Kay nodded and returned his smile. But catching herself relaxing under his unexpected charm, she reminded herself to keep the conversation on a professional level. "Even a small window can help someone work better. Do you have windows in your National City plant?" His business mask was once more in place and Kay felt a twinge of regret at the success of her tactic.

"No, we don't have windows in our plant," he answered. "The building was built during a time when windows were considered superfluous to modern design. And as it still fills the needs of the company quite well, I trust you won't recommend we build a new one."

"I doubt we will," Kay said, looking straight into his eyes. "We're used to working with less than optimal conditions and can usually find satisfactory solutions within available resources. Now, may I see last month's figures?"

Huntingdon was silent for a moment before he handed her a sheaf of papers. "The figures are only slightly down from the month before, but my advisors—who are supposed to know such things—assure me that something must be done to turn them around."

"And it's up to me to decide what that is," she said.

"Exactly."

The trip to National City took half an hour and Kay struggled to keep the conversation on a business level. But in the confines of the car they somehow got on a first-name basis, and Burke took it to mean he was then free to ask personal questions. She managed to evade most of them without being too blunt, but he did weasel her marital and family status out of her.

The tour was long but cool. Fortunately for Kay, the air-conditioning in the huge gray building was able to keep up with the heat generated by the machines, because with Burke constantly at her side, she had enough trouble keeping cool.

She did manage to talk with several of the department heads as well as some of the workers themselves. Later, Burke realized his presence made it difficult for his employees to speak freely with Kay and after that he stayed in the background.

Burke stood and watched her last interview. She was in deep conversation with Mr. Johnson, foreman of the swing shift, who had done impressive work under difficult conditions. He was a handsome young man with a delightful sense of humor and her laughter was often heard during their discussion.

Glancing up, she saw Burke, his arms crossed in front of him, watching her with an agitated glint in his eyes. His eyebrows were lowered in a frown.

Deciding he was tired of—and unused to—being in the background, she motioned him over and introduced him to the black-haired foreman.

Burke exchanged polite greetings and shook his hand, but Kay could tell by the set of his jaw that he was not in the best of moods. "Are you finished here?" he asked.

"I was just coming to tell you . . ." Her voice trailed off when she saw the look in his eyes. He was angry at her—but for what?

Mr. Johnson was standing near them nervously shifting his weight from foot to foot. "I'll get that report to you on Monday, ma'am," he said.

"What report is that?" Burke demanded. The younger man opened his mouth, but no sound came out.

"Mr. Johnson is going to write up what he has done here in his shop, under difficult conditions, to help keep production from falling too far. I could learn more from a report than from just talking with him for an hour," Kay explained.

"How soon can that report be ready, Johnson?" Burke asked tersely.

Johnson remained apprehensive but he managed to say, "Tomorrow morning, Mr. Huntingdon. But tomorrow's Saturday."

"I'll be working in my office. I want that report on my desk by eleven," Burke said.

"Yes, sir."

Kay wondered what the rush might be, then decided he wanted to read it before she did. She started to protest about his autocratic control of her project, but Burke cut her words off with a firm hand on her elbow. "It's time to leave, Dr. Pagel."

He led her to his car, barely acknowledging the goodnights from passing employees on the way. At the car he opened the door for her, then closed it with a decided snap. Getting in his side, he put the key in the ignition and sat still for a full minute with his hands on the steering wheel before he finally said, "If you need any reports from my employees, you can ask *me* for them."

"Pardon me, Mr. Huntingdon!" she said sarcastically. "But when he offered to write up what he'd done, I thought it would be of enormous help. I merely said yes."

"*All* reports, including Johnson's, go through me, is that understood?"

"As long as I get them." Her doubt that she would was clearly evident in her voice.

"You will."

He started the car and they said little on the drive back to Southey's offices. When they arrived, Burke opened the door and began to accompany her.

"Thank you, Burke, but I can find the way to my car by myself. There are only three cars in the parking lot: one is yours, one is a 'Z,' and one is mine. I don't think I'll have any problems."

"Kay, it's getting dark and that section of the lot is lit by only one streetlight. I'll accompany you."

Not wanting to argue with him after a long, tiring day, she acquiesced and walked with him. On the way she said, "I'll have the preliminary analysis ready by Tuesday, but I'll need to study Johnson's report before I can give any final recommendations. He has some excellent ideas."

"I'll look forward to it."

"If the rest of the analysis, design, and testing go well, we might be able to implement the training in three months. Then our part in this will be over and Pagel Associates can be out of your way!"

He nodded but said nothing as he helped her into her car, then stood watching as she drove out of the lot. In her rearview mirror she thought she saw that same unusual smile she'd seen earlier playing around his lips, but she was too far away to be sure.

Kay was weary. On her drive home she tried to put the disturbing Burke Huntingdon from her mind, but it proved an impossible task. Her mind was trained to analyze anything out of the ordinary, and Burke Huntingdon was certainly that!

It was easy, now that he was nowhere near her, to dismiss her reaction to him as tension she had built up worrying about the Southey account. After Huntingdon had sent Gloria and Steve back, she'd been furious. She'd only planned to lay down the law with respect to her employees and send over two other training designers—it was only after she'd met him that she'd decided to take on the job herself.

Shaking her head to clear it of the difficult man, she tried to concentrate on that night's dinner. A succulent piece of baked chicken, liberally sprinkled with tarragon, sounded good. The thought of the fresh asparagus she had bought the night before came to mind and she smiled—what a delicious reward for a trying day!

She parked her car in the garage. When she opened the door, she heard the faint ringing of her telephone, and grabbing her purse and briefcase, ran up the stairs to her condominium. Once inside, she dumped her burdens in a chair and answered the phone with a breathless "Hello?"

"Kay? This is Sally. Are you all right?" the soft friendly voice asked.

"Hi, Sally. I'm fine—I just ran up the stairs to answer the phone."

"Sorry for the bad timing. Listen, I called to ask a favor."

"Name it!" Kay said, pleased to be able to do something for the woman who had given her brother such happiness.

"That's dangerous!" Sally laughed. "But I promise not

to ask you to house Davy's lizard collection! What I *do* need, though, is somewhere to hide a present for Davy till his birthday. My dad in Detroit sent out a train set for him, but the little stinker saw it delivered and won't stop pestering me about what's in the box. I finally told him it was for you and you had it delivered here because you wouldn't be home."

"Of course you can hide it here. I know Davy couldn't possibly let that box alone for the next two months! When do you want to bring it by?"

"Would tomorrow be okay?" Sally asked. "I've got to go to a luncheon for my club anyway so I'll stop by about three. How does that sound?"

"Sounds fine. But don't expect me to be too elegant. I'll be refinishing my grandmother's nightstand."

"I wasn't expecting sequins and satin!" Sally said, laughing. "See you tomorrow."

After hanging up the phone, Kay kicked off her shoes and sat down, the thought of her nephew making her smile. But the dear little brown-haired, brown-eyed boy's face in her mind slowly changed to the face of a golden-haired man with startlingly blue eyes.

What was she going to do about Burke? Already she could feel him taking over—though, so far, it had been on a business level. Her body's reaction to him was frightening and her turmoil bothered her—it was certainly not something she'd ever dealt with in the past. Men had always been pleasant, if temporary, companions. Her interest in her schoolwork and career had always lasted, while her relationships had faded like last summer's brightly colored blouse.

She shook herself and stood up, stretching toward the ceiling. Feeling better, she went to the kitchen and opened a new bottle of Chardonnay.

The cork made a satisfying "pop" and she smiled. Digging out her largest bubble glass from the back of the cupboard, she poured herself a healthy portion of the California beverage and toasted the coming weekend.

Weekends usually found her at her office, working long hours. But this one was hers to enjoy, and she promised herself not to think about Southey Manufacturing the entire time. And she certainly wouldn't think of Burke Huntingdon!

CHAPTER TWO

Despite her good intentions, Burke Huntingdon was almost the first thing Kay thought of the next morning. What was it about him that she found so disturbing? She yawned and shook her head—she wasn't going to dwell on it.

The drizzle outside forced her to change her plans and she'd have to refinish her nightstand in the kitchen, but that didn't lower her unusually high spirits. She even found herself singing as she brushed her hair up into a topknot to keep it out of her way.

Discovering an old, shrunken gold-and-blue T-shirt, she put it on quickly, and then found an equally old pair of cutoff jeans. Looking at herself in the mirror, she made a wry face at all the tight shirt and short cutoffs revealed, then laughed, thinking Ric would even be willing to miss a Padre game if he could see her now!

After spreading newspapers on the kitchen floor, she carefully brought out the old nightstand and removed its drawer pull, hinges, and doorknob; the vacuum was close at hand to clean up the dust. Unaware of the hours that passed, she sanded it down with successively finer grades of steel wool.

Around three o'clock she sat back on her heels with a satisfied sigh: the sanding was finished, but then a groan escaped her when she saw the mess she'd made. Grabbing the vacuum cleaner, she started in on the fine, powderlike dust that had gotten everywhere. She'd almost finished vacuuming herself off when she heard the faint sound of the doorbell above the noise.

Remembering Sally, she yelled, "Come on in!" and kept on vacuuming the right leg of her short cutoffs. She heard someone approach and turned to greet Sally with a wide smile. There, leaning against her kitchen counter, was Burke Huntingdon.

"Burke!" she yelped, frozen to the floor in shock as she stood staring at him, the nozzle of the vacuum sucking loudly at her T-shirt, exposing the flat, tanned expanse of her midriff. Finally she gathered enough presence of mind to step on the "off" switch. His eyes had slowly descended over her form, so well revealed by her informal clothes and the vacuum's suction. An appreciative gleam was in his eyes when they returned to her face.

"Good afternoon," he said, his voice deeper, yet softer, than she had remembered it. "I brought by Johnson's report. You seemed anxious to get it." The short sleeves of his casual white knit top emphasized the well-developed muscles of his arms, while the smooth material followed the lines of his wide chest. Both the top and his snug-fitting jeans were damp from the rain.

Giving herself a mental shake, she said, "Thanks. I won't have time to go over it this weekend, but I'll get to it first thing Monday morning." She indicated the mess in the kitchen, a militant light in her eye daring him to disparage her for thinking the nightstand more important than Southey. "Would you like some coffee or a glass of wine?"

She laughed at his skeptical look and explained, "The coffee maker's been covered and the wine's in the refrigerator, so neither one will taste of paint dust!"

"Coffee sounds fine, if it's not too much trouble." His smile made the blood tingle in her veins.

"It's no problem; besides, I need some myself." She uncovered the coffee maker and put in a filter before opening the refrigerator.

"I don't use cream," he said, misinterpreting her actions.

"Cream? No, I know . . . oh, you thought I was getting some cream?" She smiled warmly when he nodded. "No, I grind my own coffee beans and they stay freshest when they're refrigerated."

"Seems like a lot of work to go through for something as simple as coffee," he commented, walking over to her. "Do you need some help?"

He stood close to her and her nerves cried out in anticipation of his touch. But she shook her head and forced herself to measure out the coffee calmly, saying, "Simple? You won't think so after you've tasted *my* coffee! It's superb!"

After the beans were ground to a fine powder, she started the coffee, and had begun rewrapping the coffee bag when he reached over and took it from her.

"That's the simple part—let me do it." After replacing the bag in the refrigerator, he returned to her side.

As she watched the coffee dripping into the pot, Kay tried to ignore her body's reaction to this man, yet she wanted to remain friendly with him. Even before they had met, she'd been intrigued by the man Gloria and Steve had told her so much about. She realized that he had interested her, partly at least, because of the increasing boredom she felt when with men like Ric Adler. Ric certainly never made her blood race through her veins and her nerves clamor for his touch!

"That looks old," Burke said, indicating the nightstand. "Did you buy it at a yard sale? I hear great bargains can be found at those things." His voice caressed her body as it flowed over her.

"No, my grandmother gave me a pair of them. I've already finished the other one—it's in my bedroom."

"I'd like to see it sometime." His eyes were half closed and the phantom smile hovered around his lips as he watched her reaction. The smile grew to a grin when her eyes widened at the not-so-subtle implication.

The coffeepot gave a last snort before it sat quietly, its duty done, and Kay eagerly changed the subject. "The coffee's ready."

"Where do you keep your cups?" he asked, looking around trying to guess which cupboard they might be in. He pointed to one next to the sink. "This one?"

She nodded, surprised at his accurate guess, watching as he pulled out two green mugs. Not knowing why, she gave silent thanks that, only last week, she had broken the last of the Charger mugs Ric had given her.

"Careful, it's hot," she warned, handing him a full mug of steaming black brew.

He looked at the mug and then at Kay.

His eyes never left her, their intensity making her search for something else to say. Her eyes lit on the dining-room table. "Would you like to sit down?"

Sitting close to her at the table, he casually put a hand on the back of her chair and she swallowed with difficulty. Licking her dry lips, she said, "Would you like some cookies?" and started to stand.

"No, thank you," he answered, his hand resting lightly on her shoulder to restrain her from rising.

Kay sat back down. His hand trailed down her arm a few inches as he removed his restraint. She felt the tingle of its passage even after he had stopped touching her.

His eyes were crinkled at the edges as he sat back, smiling warmly at her. She was unreasonably disappointed when he began talking about business.

"When Johnson came by this morning, he said you asked him some very perceptive questions yesterday. You certainly impressed the poor fellow."

"And that surprises you?" Kay asked, her breathing quickening as his eyes swept down over her once again.

"It does. The contract with your company was already signed when ESSCO bought Southey. I would have preferred to let the in-house people have some more time, but when you're trying to convince the employees that earth-shaking changes aren't coming, you don't start by canceling major contracts," Burke said, watching her face closely.

Taking a deep breath, she said, "Pagel Associates has an excellent reputation with the companies in San Diego. I don't understand why you feel we can't do the job." Her lips were dry again and she unconsciously licked them. The light in his eyes warmed. She was starting to have trouble thinking coherently.

"You've been dealing mostly with management-level people," he said, leaning closer to her. She could feel his breath tease the wisps of hair around her ears and she trembled ever so slightly. "You haven't dealt with production-line problems, and that's the crux of Southey's troubles." He leaned still further toward her, his hand resting on the table in front of her; it seemed so very near.

She swallowed. "Would you like some more coffee?" she asked, quickly rising and taking refuge at the counter. As she leaned against the cool laminate, her equilibrium began to return; but suddenly she felt his hand burn a trail down her back, and unthinkingly she turned and found herself crushed in his arms, his mouth open and hungry as it descended onto hers.

Conscious thought retreated as her senses rejoiced in their liberation. Every part of her, including some unknown and unguessed, came alive to the sensation of his moist lips sliding over hers with sensuous deliberation, tasting each tiny contour of her mouth while his teasing tongue lightly flicked her sensitive lower lip.

No kiss had ever drawn such delights from her own body. Staccato notes of pure energy danced along her arms and they twined around his neck of their own volition.

His kiss deepened, her teeth parting naturally as her inner rhythm took on new harmonies, new chords. His tongue explored her mouth, the slight roughness causing a thrilling friction when the tops of their tongues met and stroked. His tongue continued its passage and, sliding underneath hers to the slick moist smoothness of her mouth's deepest hidden places, started a deep burning within her. She felt light tremors pulse down his spine and she tightened her own embrace in response.

His hands sent quivering electricity through her body as they roamed freely over her. Wherever his fingers pressed into her skin through the soft cotton of her shirt, tiny explosive charges were set off. Suddenly his hands closed over her breasts, his thumbs slowly tracing the peak of the voluptuous mounds until she groaned with desire at the cannon fire his actions sent to the innermost part of her womanhood. She leaned closer into him, leaving the cool rationality of the counter behind.

His mouth left hers to kiss a path to her ear, where he seemed content to nibble and take tiny licks, a devastating attack on her already storm-tossed pulse.

"Ah, Kay, what you do to me. I would have dismissed those others sooner if I'd known about their president. . . ." His voice trailed off, but his words had been enough to jar her rationality from its hiding place.

What was she doing? Pulling back from his arms, she shook her head to clear it. Her mind was crawling back up to its normal state, but it was a slow process. The fog in her brain was thick as gelatin, but there was no doubt that rationality would win the difficult struggle. *This man's a client, for God's sake!*

Instantly, in a reversal of Pygmalion, the warm, alive woman Burke had held in his arms turned to cold, unyielding marble. But as he stepped back, the gold eyes that watched him were not entirely free of the passion they had held only a moment before. The eyelids were still weighed down by vestiges of desire and her lips were slightly swollen and hadn't yet lost the deep pink his kiss had given them.

She wanted to curse and damn him for what he had done, but in all fairness, she knew she could not. She'd been as much to blame as he for what happened, so she could only stand and stare at him, half reproachful, half in wonder at the feelings he had called into being. In that brief moment of suspended time, as she gazed long and deeply into the fathomless depths of his lapis eyes, she thought him a wizard, magician, sorcerer. Who else could have caused the temblors that had permanently altered her inner landscape? Who else but a creature of arcane powers could have made her blood boil and shown her a world she had not suspected existed?

The doorbell rang, returning her to the kitchen, but she couldn't move to answer it. The bell rang again and she saw Burke's eyebrow arch in question—why wasn't she answering the door?

Just as she started to awaken from her mysterious daze, Sally's voice came from the living room. "Kay? It's me! Don't get up from your work, I'll just put this in the clo—" Her words and her small, birdlike body came to a halt as she rounded the suspended cabinets that had shielded Burke and Kay from view. Her dark eyes darted from one to the other, the situation clearly intriguing her. Burke moved back from Kay, which only served to emphasize how close he'd been standing to her.

"I'm sorry, Kay. I didn't mean to interrupt," she chirped, unsure of the man's status, yet instinctively respecting anyone who could break her sister-in-law's habitual composure.

"Interrupting? Nonsense, Sally!" Kay cried. She mentally grimaced at the high-pitched, cracking sound of her voice. A deep breath helped, and she started again. "Sally, this is Burke Huntingdon of Southey Manufacturing. He stopped by to deliver a report. Burke, this is Sally Pagel, my sister-in-law and also my dearest friend."

They exchanged greetings, Sally's eyes twinkling roguishly as she looked from Burke to her sister-in-law. A laugh bubbled up inside of Kay at Sally's resemblance to her own five-year-old, but she did wonder what the tiny woman was up to.

The big box Sally had lugged in and propped up next to the counter started to slide. Kay leaped at the chance to escape.

"Here, let me take that for you," she offered, gripping the cumbersome package awkwardly and dragging it out of the kitchen. It took her nearly ten minutes to bully the package into her closet; when she came back, both occupants had wide grins on their faces and the suspicious looks of conspirators.

"I've invited Burke to our picnic tomorrow," Sally said, causing a large, tight knot to grip Kay's stomach. "Davy would be so pleased to have someone there who hasn't seen his kittens. He's so proud of them," she told Burke. "That's why we're celebrating—my son has decided a party for the tiny things was an absolute necessity."

"It sounds delightful, Sally," Burke said, his voice low and pleasant. "Is there anything you'd like me to bring?" His words were directed at Sally, but his blue gaze was on Kay as she stood in the doorway poised like a runner ready to flee.

Sally grinned and shook her head. "Just yourself—and maybe some sunshine! But there's plenty of room in the house if the weather doesn't clear up."

Sally looked inordinately pleased with herself, Kay thought disgustedly. Putting on an overly bright smile, she said, "How nice. Would you like some coffee, Sally? I just made it a few min—a little while ago." Her words faltered as she realized she had no idea how much time had passed.

"No, thanks, I've got to run," her sister-in-law answered. There was no hiding Sally's curiosity over Kay's ruffled composure, but it would have to wait for another time. "See you both tomorrow." And with a quick wave, she was gone.

"You don't have to go tomorrow," Kay told him,

34

though her eyes wouldn't meet his. The cabinet over his right shoulder suddenly seemed fascinating. "It's just an unexciting family picnic, after all."

"But I want to go, Kay." He walked over to her and held her chin in a light grip, forcing her to look at him. "You should know even executives need a day of fun, now and then."

"No doubt. But this isn't a sophisticated cocktail party, it's a family picnic! You'll be bored within an hour." She fought the urge to lean forward into the hard warmth of his chest.

"Oh, I don't think I'll be bored," he answered, his blue eyes sparkling as if he could see her internal struggles.

She chewed on her lower lip in vexation. What about Allen? What would Burke say when he met her brother? She would *not* allow him to embarrass Allen—even if he was an important client. But the invitation hadn't been hers, so she couldn't tell him not to go.

Pulling back from his grasp, she said, "Very well. Sally said to be there around twelve thirty."

"Good. I'll come by here just after twelve to pick you up." A smile lurked at the back of his eyes as his hand dropped. He walked through the living room to the front door and reached for the doorknob, but turned back toward her, his eyes holding laughter—and something more. "Thanks for the coffee—and you were right, it wasn't simple." He left then without giving her a chance to reply.

Going to the table to clear away the two mugs, she sat her trembling body down instead. Burke was right; the word "simple" did not apply to what had happened that afternoon.

For years she'd devoted herself to her studies and then to her work. In the three years since she'd started Pagel Associates, most of her time and energy had gone into her company. She'd dated, of course, and there'd been Matt, but no one had ever been able to reach that tucked-away part of her being the way Burke had.

But what exactly *had* Burke touched off? If her body kept it up, she was going to have a very difficult time of it these next few months.

Kay bit her lower lip, but then an impish grin lifted the corners of her mouth. These new feelings were exciting, not just in the physical sense, but in the sense of uncovering a whole new facet of herself. Surely it wouldn't hurt to find out just a *little* more? And yet the man was a client—what was she going to do?

Those same words were echoed the next day at her nephew's picnic after Sally had drawn her into the kitchen while Burke was occupied admiring Davy's new kittens.

"What am I going to do? The man's a client!"

With short, pecking strokes, Sally patted roast-beef spread onto thick slices of sourdough bread. "You've run into this problem before and haven't had any trouble dealing with it," she answered, adding, "I'm sorry I invited him if he makes you uncomfortable, but yesterday it looked as if you didn't mind him at all."

"*That's* the problem," Kay said, exasperated. "Whenever men have made passes in the past—clients or not—it's always been easy to freeze them out. But this time even a chill won't come."

Kay watched Burke through the kitchen window. Outside on the patio, protected from the day's surprisingly bright sun, the wobbling box gave ample testimony of the six kittens inside. Burke gently picked up one of the tiny balls of fluff and held it close to his face, the kitten's unseeing eyes shining like tiny dark marbles.

"It's so hard to put into words that don't sound trite or silly," Kay continued, "but what happened yesterday *wasn't* just a pass. There was something more . . . but it doesn't matter, does it? I've got a job to do and when it's over, that will be the last I see of Burke Huntingdon. Any other feelings don't—and can't—enter into it."

"Kay, I know you don't like the idea of any kind of personal relationship with men you meet through your work," Sally said softly. "But don't throw away a chance at happiness because you're attracted to a man with whom you happen to have a professional relationship."

"Happiness? Aren't you jumping the gun a little? And he's not just a man I happen to know professionally—he's a client, Sally!"

The tiny woman shook her head as she put the finishing touches on their sandwiches. "You know I met Allen when he was a student and I was a teaching assistant at college. But that didn't stop either of us when we realized we loved each other—when two people love each other, that love is worth breaking any rules for."

"Happiness and now love! Love has nothing to do with what happened yesterday," Kay said flatly. Now Burke was throwing a bright red ball to her nephew, who was giggling in delight. The man looked disturbingly fit in his casual sport shirt and corduroy jeans. "It was new and exciting, and a little scary, but it wasn't love. He's just very good at that sort of thing. How could it be love? We only met on Friday!"

A glance at her sister-in-law caught a secret little smile and Kay added, "And don't you dare say, 'Methinks she doth protest too much!'"

"Why would I say a thing like that?" was the innocent reply.

A sound from the garage broke in on their conversation at the same time that Davy, with a broad smile, broke off playing ball and ran toward the house shouting, "Daddy! Daddy!" at the top of his lungs. Burke followed him into the kitchen and stepped close to Kay, his arm going around her waist to escort her. Deep-seated embers flared at his touch, throwing all of her logical, practical resolutions to the winds. He remained close to her as they all went into the garage to greet Kay's brother.

As they walked through the door, the side door of a large blue van slid back to reveal Allen Pagel. His hair was a shade darker than Kay's and his eyes appeared hazel rather than amber, but the family resemblance between the two was strong. His nose, straight and narrow, was the only feature which differed markedly from his sister's.

He had positioned his wheelchair close to the opening and activated the van's lift. A hum filled the air as it came into position. Allen rolled out onto it, locked his wheels, and slowly lowered himself to the ground. A wide smile was on his face as he watched his son jump up and down, waiting for the lift to bring his father to hugging level.

"Sorry I had to go in to work today. I hope I'm not too late," he said as soon as the sound from the hydraulic lift had stopped. His son flew into his arms and gave him a big squeeze. With Davy firmly perched on one knee, Allen pulled a switch and a soft whir accompanied him as his chair moved toward the kitchen door. He glanced curiously at his sister and her companion the while.

"Look, Daddy," Davy told him, "Aunt Kay brought her boyfriend! He's nice, you know. I already showed him Casper and George and—"

Three of the adults laughed at the child's enthusiasm and missed Kay's embarrassment at Davy's calling Burke her boyfriend. She had looked at him quickly, but he was smiling and laughing with the others and apparently hadn't noticed.

"Allen," Kay said once they had all settled on the back patio, cool drinks in hand, "I'd like you to meet Burke Huntingdon. He's—"

"—a friend," Burke finished. "How do you do, Allen."

Frowning at him, Kay completed the introduction. "Burke, this is my brother, Allen Pagel." Her fierce pride was clearly evident in her voice, tinged as it was with a touch of belligerence daring anyone to say anything against him.

"How do you do, Burke," Allen said, his voice a pleasant baritone. "It's nice to finally meet a friend of Kay's."

"That's not true!" Kay cried. "You've met Gloria!"

Allen chuckled good-naturedly at having sparked a reaction in his sister. "Well, Burke, at least she's willing to show you off to us. Sounds like a good sign."

"Allen!" Kay exclaimed, mortified by his assumption.

Burke laughed, a deep rumbling from his chest. "I'm afraid it's not as good as it sounds—your wife invited me!"

"Now, you two, stop teasing Kay," Sally said with a twinkle in her eyes as she watched Burke gaze at Kay with something remarkably close to tenderness in his eyes. "Davy, hop down off your father's lap and help me get the food on the table before we all starve!"

"Aunt Kay! Did you bring the p'tato salad?" Davy asked anxiously.

"What do you think was in that big bowl I was carrying?" she asked in return.

"Okay—I jus' wanted to make sure," he answered. Kay ruffled his hair with a laugh. He ducked away and ran into the kitchen to help his mom.

The picnic was a huge success, the laughing and talking bringing the two couples together as nothing else could. Burke sat close to Kay on the picnic bench, the length of his thigh occasionally rubbing against hers, making the heat and sparks from the friction a subliminal craving. Unconsciously she began to lean toward him, seeking the touch whenever the contact was removed for a moment. It didn't happen often.

The shadows began to lengthen and the light dim, but it wasn't until they were startled by the automatic yard light coming on that they realized how late it was.

"Would you like to go in the house?" Sally asked. "It's getting chilly out here."

"No, thanks, Sal," Kay answered, "I think we'd better

be going. I've got a long week ahead of me." She glanced meaningfully at Burke, who grinned in understanding.

On the drive home Kay and Burke continued their lazy, companionable conversation, hopping from subject to subject, unconscious of where their words took them. As the wind from the car's open window blew at her hair, Kay wondered if she should ask him in when they reached her house, but then she told herself not to worry—let him make the decision when they arrived.

The low-slung Porsche rumbled to a halt in her driveway. She watched his lithe grace through the windshield as he came around to open her side of the car and took a deep breath of his intoxicating scent as he helped her rise from her seat. He escorted Kay to her door, and after waiting for her to unlock it, followed her into the living room.

"Would you like some coffee?" She had started to walk to the kitchen, but now stopped in the middle of the floor and turned around to see what he wanted.

Burke was standing close to her and she was mesmerized by the slight movement his chest made as it rose and fell with his breathing.

"Coffee? I'm coffeed and lemonaided out." He laughed. "Didn't you mention some wine the last time I was here?"

She smiled in answer and went to get him a glass, trying to shake off his effect on her. She retrieved the chilled bottle of white wine she had opened two nights before and grabbed two glasses from the cupboard. Sitting down on the sofa next to him, she poured the pale, fragrant beverage.

Kay swirled her wine thoughtfully. Looking up into his eyes, dark with his own inner thoughts, she smiled tentatively and said, "I want to thank you for the way you reacted to Allen. Too many people start running to fetch everything for him, making him feel uncomfortable and even more self-conscious than he normally is."

"He seemed perfectly capable to me," Burke said.

His mouth curved into a gentle smile when she answered fiercely, "He is!"

"I think I would know him for your brother anywhere." He cradled her jaw in his hand, rubbing his thumb along the just below her eye, along the prominent cheekbone. "You both get that same intent look in your eyes when you're concentrating hard, as if trying to direct every extra ounce of energy to the matter. It's very flattering when you get that look and I happen to be the matter at hand."

A blush of pleasure at his words stole up her cheeks and she stuttered, "Th—thank you." The commonplace words were made uncommon by their sincerity.

"You must hold your brother in very high esteem," he said softly, watching the delightful cream of her complexion return as the rose of her blush faded. "He was probably a better brother than I was!"

Instead of the smile he had expected, his words caused a dart of pain to flash through her golden eyes. Lowering her eyes to stare at her fingers as they drew simple designs in the condensation on her wineglass, she was still and silent for a long while. Finally she raised her face and looked at him with eyes overbright from unshed tears.

"It wasn't until my father died that I really came to know my brother," she whispered.

He reached out to her, to explain by touch that she didn't have to tell him. As she shook her head, the salty droplets overflowed to fall down her cheek. "It was his strength that got me through the difficult time after my father died, though I mourned a man whom he had little cause to love."

"His father . . . ?" Burke asked, hesitating yet wanting to understand her story.

"My father could hardly stand to look at him; we rarely did things as a family. My mother spent all her time and energy on Allen, while my father spent what little time he had away from his work with me. We were like strangers in the same house." She shook her head and said, sniffing,

"This is silly." Getting up, she went to the box of Kleenex, and facing away from him, dried her eyes and gave a hearty honk into the tissue.

Returning dry eyed, she sat down next to him and finished briskly, "So you see, when the father I had idolized died, I had no one—though my mother had always let me go my own way pretty much, we'd never gotten along—and I didn't know my brother well at all. But I'd already applied for graduate school here in San Diego, so when he offered to let me stay with him and Sally, I accepted. It's the best thing I've ever done."

Silently he leaned over and poured her another glass of wine. Handing it to her, he said, "At least you've found him now. You should cherish that."

The glass was tilted up to her mouth and she looked at him through its distortion. "I do," she said softly, then quickly sipped the wine.

To break the solemn mood she had fallen into, Kay stood up suddenly and went to the stereo. "Do you mind if I put on some music?"

"Not at all, as long as it isn't New Wave," Burke said lightly. "I'm afraid that stuff's beyond the limits of my musical tolerance."

Laughing, Kay said, "I don't blame you a bit. That 'music' is the reason I finally decided to buy a condo. In my last apartment the walls were thin and my neighbors were fans of what Davy calls 'thump-thump' music. On most days it felt as if I were living in someone's chest cavity!"

Burke chuckled at the image. "It does sound remarkably like someone's erratic heartbeat. Living next to it would be Chinese torture."

"It was, believe me! I found a condo with the thickest walls I could find and promptly bought it!"

Selecting her favorite Mozart sonata, she waited until its lovely strains filled the air before returning to sit next to Burke. They both visibly relaxed as the graceful melody worked its magic.

As the silence grew, Kay was pleasantly surprised to find that it was a comfortable one. She didn't feel the slightest need to make conversation and Burke, leaning back against the sofa, his long legs stretched out before him, obviously felt the same. Her mouth curved into a slow, contented smile that was unconsciously sensuous.

In unwitting response Burke reached up and gently touched her hair. There was a lamp behind her head and its rays made her hair glow with a golden halo as tiny untamed strands caught the light.

Her nerves relaxed. Warmed by the wine, the music, and his barely perceptible touch on her hair, the structured part of her mind—the cold, rational businesswoman part—slipped away almost unnoticed. As it left, she luxuriated in the discovery of the sensual half of her nature, lamenting that the two halves of her being were not yet a complete whole.

"Do you know how beautiful you are?" he whispered.

She smiled in answer and leaned her head into his nearby hand. The hand trailed a loving line down her face, and without thinking of consequences, she kissed his palm as it passed.

His eyes, which had been as clear and blue as a mountain lake, darkened to the color of a summer storm. His lids half-closed as he leaned forward, pulling her to him at the same time. They met in a sultry, luxurious kiss.

It was a familiar kiss, yet the heat of it filled her veins with a languid fire, warming her to new depths. His lips traveled over hers again and again in successive kisses that devastated her self-control. The gentle friction of his lips sent lightning jolting through her with each kiss and a blaze began at her very core that sent out wave after wave of urgent heat. They breathed in rhythm, their short breaths lasting only as long as their lips could bear to be apart.

"Ah, Kay," he murmured as they leaned back, his dark eyes scanning her face in wonder. He closed his eyes and shook his head as if to deny what was in his mind. "Kay," he said, opening his eyes once more, "we have to talk—first."

She had to take a moment to regain her composure. "Why don't we talk in the morning, Burke?" Instinctively she knew he was about to bring up business and something inside of her balked at discussing that unwanted subject at the moment.

"All right. But we do have to talk," he said resignedly. "I'll call you tomorrow." With that he rose, and after motioning her to remain seated, kissed her lightly on the forehead. The touch of his lips felt cool on her heated skin.

"Burke?" she asked softly, a puzzled frown clouding her amber eyes as she watched him walk toward the door.

"I must go," he said, his voice unsteady. "I'll talk to you tomorrow." He looked at the golden woman seated on the couch as if for the last time until, his jaw clenching with resolve, he turned and left. The strains of the Mozart sonata muffled the sound of the door closing behind him.

CHAPTER THREE

Kay spent Monday morning trying not to look at the phone as she worked on the Southey project in her office. Her heart had jumped every time it had rung and she hadn't been able to control that errant organ. By eleven thirty Burke still hadn't called; she gave up on him.

Let that be a lesson in how to cool off forward women executives! The thought was a bitter one, but she refused to feel mortified, thinking that at least *her* reactions had been honest ones. When the sky darkened suddenly, she found it grimly satisfying.

The phone rang again. "Very good," she addressed her heart. "You barely reacted that time." But her feeling of accomplishment was short lived—her heart leaped with joy at the first sound of Burke's deep voice.

"I've been stuck in a meeting," he said by way of explanation. "Could we meet for lunch?"

"I really can't take the time, Burke," she answered, a surge of guilty satisfaction running through her at paying him back. Trying to assuage that guilt, she explained, "I've been going through Southey's reports all morning and I need to keep working on the analysis."

"We really need to talk—before you start any serious work on this project."

Her professional mind was alert at once. Over the noise of alarms ringing in her brain, she asked, "What are you saying, Burke?"

He hesitated, obviously debating with himself over what

he should tell her. "Let's meet for lunch and we'll discuss it," he said finally. "You pick the place."

Not daring to say no this time, she mentioned a well-known restaurant in Old Town, an area that had been the original Spanish settlement but was now a delightful assemblage of small shops and museums. The restaurant served extraordinary hamburger concoctions inspired by Mexican cuisine.

"I know the place," he said. "Meet you there at one."

As she hung up the phone, her secretary knocked and entered. "Kay, I don't want to disturb you," Mary Duncan said, "but I think you ought to know there's some strange guy talking with Steve and Gloria out in the parking lot."

"There's nothing unusual in that, surely," Kay said, though she knew that Mary didn't indulge in gossip. It was one of the things that made her such an excellent secretary.

"When I was going out to lunch, I overheard Gloria invite him in to talk with you, but he laughed and said that's the last thing he'd do. I just thought you'd like to know."

"Thanks, Mary, but it's probably just Jane's new husband or someone like that. I do appreciate your concern," Kay said sincerely. "Now, go on and get some lunch and try not to think of Pagel! You deserve it."

"Okay," Mary said good-naturedly, "but don't say I didn't warn you!"

An hour later Kay was walking toward Bazaar del Mundo, the collection of shops and restaurants in Old Town which also housed her destination. The clouds she had first noticed right before Huntingdon had called were now a solid, overcast gray. She had almost reached the bright awning of the restaurant when large drops began to fall, forcing her to run the last few steps to safety.

The hostess was standing behind her station looking tired but relieved that the noon rush was almost over. Her dark hair and eyes drooped with exhaustion, but when Kay walked up, she brightened considerably. She looked at Kay closely and asked, "Dr. Pagel?" At Kay's look of surprise the woman smiled broadly, her tiredness retreating for a moment. "Mr. Huntingdon has already arrived. This way, please."

She led Kay to a corner booth facing a window but isolated from the few remaining patrons. Burke stood as they approached. The hostess beamed a smile at him. "You described her very well, Mr. Huntingdon." Her voice conveyed her envy that it had been Kay—and not her—whom he had described.

When they were alone with their menus, Burke chuckled and said, "You can take the frown off your face. She's gone."

Kay turned her frown on him to quell his implication, but it was hard to remain miffed at a man whose eyes crinkled so endearingly when he smiled.

Had anyone else implied that she was jealous of a restaurant hostess, she would have been livid. But, sighing inwardly at her own susceptibility, she let the matter drop.

"What *is* it that's so important?" she asked him.

The smile disappeared and his eyes lost their glitter. But instead of answering her, he only urged her to make a selection from the menu, adding, "There'll be plenty of time to discuss business after we've eaten."

"Burke, this isn't a social lunch—I have to get back and work on that analysis."

"Kay—" he began, then stopped. Their eyes locked, azure gazing into gold, and Kay could see that something was deeply troubling him. He broke the contact and looked out the window. "Surely time spent with a client isn't wasted?"

"No, I suppose not," she conceded with a frown. What was bothering him?

A waitress, whose orange-blond hair had not been dyed recently, came to take their order, giving them a brittle smile before launching into her polite spiel. When she'd left, he turned back to face Kay, an impish smile making his eyes sparkle once again. "How's your chest coming?"

"My what?"

"Your chest—you know, that thing you were scrubbing in the middle of the kitchen."

"My *nightstand* is quite well, thank you," she answered, trying hard not to smile. "I've had to postpone working on it for a while, though, until this project is done. Southey is taking up all of my time these days."

When she mentioned the project, a dullness flashed through his eyes as if at an unsettling thought. But his mischievous smile was back quickly. "Pity," he said, the smile traveling to his eyes. "It has quite an interesting structure. And you were quite right not to hide it . . . under all that paint."

Kay blushed at the embarrassing reminder of how she had been dressed. Had his kiss been motivated solely by her clothes?

"The *nightstand* is safely tucked away in a closet," she said, an answering twinkle in her honey-colored eyes. "I couldn't let it stand out in the kitchen unprotected—so many unpleasant things could happen to it that way. Don't you agree?"

Burke gave a shout of laughter, drawing several disapproving looks. He was prevented from answering her, though, by the arrival of their appetizer—an enormous mound of tortilla chips, chili, and melted cheddar cheese, with a generous dollop of sour cream on one side and guacamole on the other. Kay took one look at that and knew she couldn't take just a bite or two as she'd planned. It was going to be steamed vegetables that night!

Burke kept putting off their business discussion. After they had finished lunch, he insisted that she accompany him on a leisurely tour of Old Town. The rain had stopped but the sky was still overcast, which explained why so few people were out that afternoon sauntering beneath the benign gaze of the old mission atop Presidio Hill.

They entered the original office of the San Diego *Union* and walked through the collection of old quoins, fonts, and presses. They ventured out behind the small museum to a isolated miniature park where stone benches sat snugly on the thick grass.

"Burke, will you get to the point?" Kay pleaded as he led her along the shaded path. She assumed they were headed to another museum, but at that moment she really didn't care. "You can't drag me all over Old Town trying to avoid saying whatever it is you want to say to me." He didn't stop and did nothing to indicate he had even heard her. "Burke!"

Stopping next to a profusely budding tree, Burke gave no warning as he pulled her into his arms and kissed her deeply. His moist lips pressed against hers and his tongue darted in tiny quicksilver flashes over the sensitive inner flesh of her lips. It was remarkable, really, she thought in some distant part of her mind, how Burke's kisses were so exciting and delightful and *different*. Not just different from any of the other kisses she'd had, but different from each other.

Saturday's had been a volcanic revelation, erupting inside her with explosive force. His kiss yesterday had been soft and undemanding, yet all the more sensuous for he had drunk in every drop of her mouth's sweetness.

And now, she thought absently as their tongues fenced playfully, now it was warming, like sitting in front of a fire after coming in out of the snow. She could feel the fire's warmth creeping along her veins, thawing her body from its winter of solitude.

The kiss ended and Kay drew back, looking into his half-closed eyes, trying to calm her erratically beating heart and recover her senses. Surprised to discover she was holding her breath, she let it out in a long sigh which, to her dismay, sounded like an invitation. He was not at all reluctant to accept it and his mouth covered hers once again.

They stood looking at each other for a long moment after that second kiss ended, neither of them speaking. Burke silently led her to a curved stone bench on the other side of the tree and they sat facing each other.

"Kay," Burke said, breaking the long silence between them, "how old is your company?"

She tilted her head sideways as she often did when trying to solve a puzzle and answered, "Three years. Why?"

"I need to know how long you've had to learn about the business world."

"The business world? What do you mean?" she asked, shaken from the complacency his kiss has caused. "We're not amateurs, if that's what you mean! Pagel Associates has a good, solid reputation in San Diego."

"I'm not talking about your company's reputation. . . ."

"Are you worried we'll not deliver on time?" Kay asked hotly, ignoring the burning path his hands traced on her arms. "I'm trying damnably hard to do just that, but for some reason, Southey's president keeps preventing me!"

"Kay, settle down. That's not what I'm trying to say at all." His hands held her shoulders in a firm grip. "What I *am* trying to say—and doing it badly—is that business decisions are often made without any regard for personal relationships between the same people. Do you understand that?"

"Of course I understand it. It's a basic assumpt—" Kay stopped and began again. "What decision?"

"Kay," he said, his blue eyes looking deeply into her gold ones as if trying to convey his innocence, "Southey has decided to 'back-burner' the project with Pagel." His hands instinctively tightened their hold on her shoulders as she stiffened.

50

"Back-burner our project? Why do you want to postpone it? We have a contract!"

"Believe me, right now, it's for the best," he said, dropping his hands from her shoulders and becoming absorbed in studying a nearby stone wall.

"What do you mean 'for the best'?" Kay asked him angrily. "Only last Friday you maneuvered me into taking over the project personally. And now you want to 'back-burner' it. Why don't you just say *postponed indefinitely?* In fact, why don't you just say *canceled?*" He was watching her now, watching her eyes turn metallic gold in anger; watching her chest rapidly rise and fall with her ragged breathing.

"The project is *not* canceled. We still need that work done—later."

She opened her mouth for a furious retort, then stopped. Looking at him closely, she suddenly realized he was nervous; his short, abrupt actions communicating his agitation. "Burke, what is it you *aren't* telling me?" she asked softly. "Is there some problem that involves Pagel?"

He looked shaken, as if her swift change of attack had almost thrown him off guard. "No," he finally said, "no, it doesn't involve Pagel—the reason we've back-burnered the project is strictly an internal affair, Kay. As soon as our 'problem' is taken care of, your project will be the first one reactivated. I promise you that."

Was he lying? For once she couldn't tell. He had changed swiftly—she hadn't seen the metamorphosis, only the result. His eyes were hooded; his face was an unreadable mask—the kind that comes in handy in five-card stud.

"Will you let me know if anything comes up that *does* involve Pagel?"

"Of course."

She wondered how she ever thought she could know him. He was as remote as a desert island—and as inaccessible—and completely different from the man she had come to care for at yesterday's picnic.

Thinking of the change in him, she was caught unaware when his arms captured her and his lips came down in a hard, demanding kiss. His lips crushed hers, as she squirmed and struggled to get free. She discovered herself held in an iron grip, and for the first time she knew the full power of the strength promised in his well-developed muscles.

Still, she struggled. The kiss was a command which she instinctively fought until she was finally able to break free, her palm coming up to slap him hard across his cheek.

"Damn you, Burke Huntingdon," she spat before turning and walking swiftly to her car.

"Kay! Wait!"

She ignored him.

If he'd wanted to divert her thoughts from the postponement, he'd succeeded. By the time she reached her car, she was shaking in reaction and her keys refused to go in the lock. When they fell to the ground for the second time, she leaned up against the car and took deep breaths to control her rampant nerves. Her hand was balled into a fist; the good solid fist her father had taught her.

"This is absurd," she told herself under her breath as she relaxed a bit. The keys worked the third time, and throwing her purse on the passenger seat, she drove directly home.

Once there, she ripped off her clothes piece by piece and threw them on the floor, the path of discarded clothing leading to her bedroom. Clad only in her underwear, she went to the bathroom to run a steaming hot bath, hoping it would relax her. While it was running, she phoned her office.

"Mary? Have you talked with Gloria or Steve recently?"

"I talked to Gloria about a half hour ago. Do you need something?"

"I just need to know if they mentioned having any problems with their new project this morning," she said.

"No, everything's going fine," her secretary replied.

"Good. I'm not going to be back in today," Kay told her. "Keep it under your hat, but the project with Southey has been 'back-burnered.' " Her voice conveyed her still-boiling anger at the decision. Her eyes, idly wandering around the room as she spoke, noticed her luggage tucked in the corner of the open closet. A grim smile slowly grew across her face.

"Mary, change that. Call Gloria and tell her she'll have to handle Pagel this week. I've decided to take my vacation right now, while I have the chance. You've got the number in Big Bear—tell her to call me if anything comes up—otherwise, I'll be incommunicado for a week."

"What about Brighton? You needed to talk with them."

"I'll call old man Brighton right now. What's his number?"

As soon as she'd hung up, she ran and turned off the bath water. Phoning the Brighton Plastic Company, she explained there would be a delay. Fortunately their own project was behind schedule and they were quite willing to accept a postponement.

The long, lazy bath she had planned turned into a quick shower. She dried rapidly and dressed. After pulling on a pair of khaki pants and an olive-and-tan plaid short-sleeved shirt, she dragged her luggage out and feverishly began to pack.

Confusion and outrage warred in her brain. How had her body chosen such a man? Why had her heart remained untouched for so many years only to awaken for the president of a client company? He was a businessman and the businessmen she had known would stop at nothing for their own advancement in the business world. She mustn't lose sight of that.

Trying to fold a slippery silk blouse, she stopped suddenly, allowing it to slip out of the neat folds once again.

But hadn't she done the same thing when she started her company? The thought intruded on her diatribe against Burke, forcing her to acknowledge that perhaps she'd behaved in much the same way in her struggle to establish Pagel Associates. But knowing she had behaved that way didn't excuse Burke's actions. She would still have to remember he was a client.

It was approaching four thirty when she finally managed to pack everything she needed into her trunk. She was surprised at how little there was: aside from the requisite changes of clothing, she'd added a few books and the reports from Southey. A leisurely glance through them wouldn't hurt, she'd told herself. And, after arranging for a neighbor to pick up her mail, carefully checking the windows and doors and faucets, and unplugging her appliances, she was ready to leave.

Backing out of her garage, she was watching the fence to her right when a flash of red caught her eye and she slammed on her brakes—and felt the pedal go all the way to the floor.

As she heard the tires from Burke's Porsche squeal, she grabbed the emergency brake and brought her car to a halt inches from his car door. A telltale warning light on her dashboard glared up at her.

"Just what the hell are you doing?" she yelled, the car door slamming behind her.

"What am *I* doing? What about you? Do you always try to run over people you don't like?" he countered, his own car door slamming with equal force.

She started to reply and then couldn't. Her first response was to tell him she didn't dislike him at all, but she certainly wasn't in the mood to tell him that!

Electing to say nothing, she knelt down next to her car and peered underneath the chassis. An oily fluid was dripping out of a rubber hose and a four-foot trail of it gave an uncompromising clue as to what had happened.

Burke's face appeared on the other side, his forehead

cut off from view by the frame of the car. He looked at her through the drip and said, "Your brake line burst."

"No kidding." She got up and leaned against the car, crossing her arms in front of her. Now what was she going to do?

He came around the back of her car and stood next to her. "I'm glad to know you weren't *trying* to run me down."

She glanced at him disgustedly and said nothing.

"Well, what are you going to do?" he asked, ignoring her obvious wish that he would just go away. "Do you belong to triple-A?"

"Yes, I belong to triple-A, and no, I don't want to call them. I was just leaving on a nice vacation in Big Bear and right now I'm not in the mood for solicitous company presidents. Why don't you call me in six months or so?"

"Big Bear? Why Big Bear? You can't ski in May."

"I have a cabin there."

"Does someone have a car you could borrow?" he asked.

Putting her hand to her forehead, she answered, "Look, Burke, I appreciate—"

"Kay, why won't you let me apologize for my behavior this afternoon? I'm trying to, you know."

She looked at him for a long moment and then said, "Okay, you're forgiven. Now let me . . . what are you doing?"

Burke had reached past her into her car and snatched the keys from the ignition. He opened her car's trunk and whistled low. Giving a shrug, he went to the Porsche and folded down the rear seat before opening the hatch. The combination formed a surprisingly roomy trunk and he began transferring her luggage to it.

"Burke! I can't take your car!" Kay cried.

"You're not going to take it. I'm driving you up there myself," he told her as he snugly packed in her two soft-sided pieces of luggage. When he picked up the Southey papers, he grinned at her but said nothing.

"This is ridiculous—you can't just commandeer me!"

"Don't you want to go to Big Bear?" he asked silkily.

"Of course I do! But I can't let you take me," Kay said, a note of panic creeping into her voice. "Burke—it's three hours away—it'll be midnight before you get back."

"I'll worry about that when the time comes."

The Porsche's hatch closed with a solid sound; to Kay it sounded like a prison door closing behind her. But was she inside or was she being set free?

"Let's try and push your car back into the garage. If we can't, we'll have to call a tow truck." He waited for her to get positioned at the passenger door before releasing the brake.

"Okay—push!"

The car went into the garage with little trouble. When the garage door had been closed and locked, Kay looked at him and said, "I really shouldn't be letting you do this, you know."

"Nonsense. And you can thank me later," he said with a grin. "Let's go."

When they finally left, they ran right into rush-hour traffic. Creeping west along Interstate 8, they spent half an hour reaching the northbound freeway that would take them most of the way to Big Bear.

To drown out the noises of the slow-moving traffic, Burke put a cassette in the tape deck. Kay looked at him quizzically as the strains of a Mozart sonata filled the car's interior. It was the same sonata she had chosen Sunday night.

"That's one of my favorite pieces," she said. "But you already know that. Are you trying to tell me something?"

He grinned in response. Quickly he glanced at her before returning his eyes to the traffic. The glance held more than she'd have thought possible for so brief a time.

Yet it had asked her for both her understanding and forgiveness. She chuckled and smiled her assent.

"Now that my maneuver's worked, you can change the tape if you want—there are some others in that lunch pail behind my seat," he offered.

"As much as I love that sonata, I have to admit it does seem a bit out of place. What else have you got?" She reached for the container and opened it up. There, in neat rows, was a substantial collection of cassette tapes. "Why a lunch pail? They make hundreds of different carriers for these things."

"Would you believe I can't afford it?" She grinned and shook her head. "Didn't think you would. Well, how about this—if you were a thief, would you break a window and risk arrest for somebody's lunch?"

"Not a bad idea. Let's see what you've got—how about some jazz?"

"Great," Burke said as he drove in the intricate ballet steps that would take him from one freeway to another.

An hour later they were forced to stop while police and crews cleared away debris from an overturned semi. That delay, coupled with stopping in San Bernardino for a late dinner, prevented their arriving in Big Bear until after eleven.

Twice on the way up the mountain Kay found herself nodding off to sleep, but Burke seemed able to find his way without her directions, so she finally curled sideways in the seat and fell asleep. The drive up with Burke had altered her feelings for him. In her dreams she was willing to admit she liked him, liked him more than any other man, in fact. But she didn't want to explore her mind and heart beyond that.

"Kay," Burke said gently, "Kay. Wake up."

"I'm awake. Is something wrong?" she asked groggily.

"No, nothing's wrong, but we're almost to Big Bear City and I don't know how to get to your house." Kay gave him mumbled directions and fell back to sleep.

The crunching of the Porsche's tires over the graveled driveway announced their arrival as Kay yawned and stretched.

"Good thing I keep it habitable," she said as they walked up the stairs to the front door. "I can worry about unpacking tomorrow."

Entering behind him in the dark, she closed her eyes and took a deep breath, inhaling the scent of the pine. She exhaled in a sigh and suddenly found herself swept up in strong arms.

Taken off guard, she was too startled to protest when his demanding lips covered hers. By the time she thought to stop him, a delicious languor had set in and she discovered her arms were already twined around his neck as if she were a vine getting life from the solid tree of his body.

His tongue was exploring her mouth, refusing any resistance and teasing her own tongue with sparks of fire. His hands freely caressed her body in long, sensuous strokes, leaving a trail of tingling heat wherever they traveled. She pressed close to him and felt the hardness of his body and his desire for her.

His mouth left her lips and his molten kisses flowed down her neck to the scented valley between her breasts. His hands had released her blouse and it fell away to the floor as he undid the front clasp of her bra and immediately imprisoned her full breasts in his hands, the pink nipples exquisitely tortured under his unrelenting thumbs. Kay groaned at the lightning that shot down to her womanhood and she felt a smoldering fire begin to flame.

He lifted her in his arms and carried her up the short flight of stairs to the loft, gently laying her down on the king-sized bed. In her impassioned state the down comforter beneath her felt like a cloud.

Her hands had unbuttoned his shirt and rippled down his back, conveying her desire. He groaned deep in his throat and once more trailed kisses down her neck to her breasts. Her body was in an agony of waiting as it readied itself for him. But then, without warning, Burke drew back and sat up, taking deep breaths as if he had been underwater drowning and had just broken into the air.

"Burke?" Kay cried out in an agonized question. Her body was burning with the passion he had stirred up and now he was holding her back from that glorious promise of release. "Why did you stop?" Her voice cracked with its confusion and hurt and she cringed at the piteous sound it made in the darkness. God, how she wanted him! She drew a long, slow line down his back, trying to convince him to return to her. But though she felt his body shiver in response, he shook his head.

"Kay, not here, not now," he answered. His voice was hoarse and drawn. Obviously he still wanted her as much as she wanted him, but he had stopped. Why?

"Why not here? Why not now?"

"Damn it, woman, you ask a lot of questions!"

"And I'm going to keep asking them until I get some answers!" Piqued, she slipped under the covers and pulled them up to her chin. He was *not* going to see her body trembling with its desire for him! "You're not getting cold feet, are you?"

"Don't be ridiculous. I'm thirty-five years old!"

"Then why? Did you you suddenly discover an aversion to brown-haired women?" When he didn't answer immediately, she added in a whisper, "Or did you suddenly discover an aversion to me?"

At that he turned around and looked at her, a strangely tender look in his eyes. "No, Kay, I didn't develop an aversion to women with hair the color of the finest honey." He smiled in the way that melted her heart and reached up to brush away gently some wisps of hair from her face. "For the first time in my life I'm finding that I want more than just a brief relationship. It frightens the hell out of me, Kay, and yet at the same time I want everything between us to be special."

Kay ignored the flight of her heart as it soared on the

wings of his words. Coaxing it back into its cage, she refused to look too deeply for the reasons she had allowed Burke to get so near to her heart, but the cynicism of her business training still ruled her brain enough for her to believe that, for all his talk of relationships, it would end when the contract with Southey ended.

"Burke, don't play games with me. I fully understand how these things are conducted. When the contract's over . . ."

He didn't let her finish. Grabbing her shoulders, he pulled her to him, close enough for her to see his eyes glittering in the darkness. "Kay Pagel, when this report is finally done and you're free of contracts and projects, you will not be free of me! This is *not* a game between us!"

"No, it's not a game," she said quietly, his words bringing back her rationality in full force.

"How many men have you let get close to you?" he asked in a voice just above a whisper. "Not many, I'd wager. But you've got so much to give!"

Kay snorted and sat up in bed, holding the sheet close to her. "So much to give? What good does it do me? Matt couldn't stand the competition I represented and left in a big hurry, and after my father died, I discovered how much more he had kept from me than he had given. What good does such misdirected love do?"

When Burke put a hand up to wipe away the silent tears that had fallen down her face, she tried to look away, but he put an adamant hand on her chin and forced her to look at him while he dried her tears with the edge of the sheet.

He kissed her gently, his lips barely pressing against hers. "Kay, why don't you get undressed and go to bed; I'll sleep on the sofa tonight. And you do have a great deal to give. You're a fine businesswoman, just don't lose the woman in the business, okay?"

When she would have answered him, he stopped her with another kiss and got off the bed. She heard him searching around for blankets and a pillow, then listened to the silence. In the late night's darkness his words had soothed and she felt there might be some truth in them. But another part of her mind warned that after he'd gone in the morning, she would consider this night as nothing more than an enchanted dream.

CHAPTER FOUR

Blinking in confusion, Kay woke with the sun filtering across her face. She tucked her head under the pillow to escape, but the delicious smell of fresh coffee brought her out again.

She sat up in bed and listened for noise from the kitchen. Rewarded with a satisfying rattle, she flung off the comforter to get out of bed and then flung it right back over her. Her clothes were all still packed away! And her suitcases were probably still piled by the door—or wherever Burke had dropped them last night. A blush accompanied that memory.

The sounds from the kitchen changed pitch and she heard Burke singing a popular song exuberantly, if not accurately. Why was he still here? She'd expected him to have returned to San Diego by now, especially after the events of night before.

She dashed to the bathroom while he was still in the kitchen and quickly started the shower going, letting the water get hot as she pinned up her hair. The two shower heads sprayed from opposite ends toward her in the center, and she let the water pound on her as if it could drive the memories of last night from her mind.

Finished, she carefully wrapped a large towel around her, glancing down at the sink as she did so. Surprisingly, two toothbrushes were neatly laid out on the counter. Next to the toothbrushes she saw the other things she had brought with her, all laid out in neat order. She sighed with exasperation; he'd unpacked while she'd slept!

Cautiously opening the bathroom door, she tried to see if Burke was sitting at the table eating his breakfast yet. She didn't see him there, but the kitchen was silent, and thinking he must have stepped outside for a moment, she walked into the bedroom.

"Aaaaah!" she cried, jumping in surprise. Burke stood beside her with a cheerful smile, holding some extra towels in one hand.

"I thought you might need these," he said.

"You nearly frightened my out of my skin!"

"Out of your towel at least," he said, his eyes briefly traveling down her.

Her equanimity was recovered along with the slipping towel. She walked to the closet and pulled on her robe as gracefully as she could manage while still keeping a firm grip on her only covering.

"I put your things away this morning," he told her, putting the towels down on the bed.

"So I noticed," she said. "Thanks." Tying the sash tightly, she started gathering clothes to wear that day. "I don't mean to sound ungrateful, but why are you still here? Aren't you desperately needed in San Diego?"

He came close to her to drop a kiss on her nose and said, "No, I'm not. I called them this morning and told them not to expect me for a week or so."

"A week!" She backed away from his closeness and tried to ignore the feelings his slight touch had sparked.

"I'd say that will be enough time," he said.

Rising to his bait, she asked, "Enough time for what?"

"We can talk after breakfast—right now, what do you say to a mushroom and cheese omelette?" he said, reaching up to tuck a fallen curl behind her ear.

She bit her lip to keep from crying out at her reaction to his touch; her skin burned with the heat of unquenched flames, but she managed to nod and say, "That sounds fine." His words sounded suspicious and she hated to be kept in the dark, but she didn't think she could hold her own with him at the moment.

He went back to the kitchen. She picked up her discarded towel from the floor, while frantically trying to think of excuses to convince him to leave. She had come to Big Bear to escape him and now he would be even closer to her than if she'd remained in San Diego! Remembering her response to him the night before, she shook her head in disbelief and sat down hard on the bed. *Kay, old girl, the man's dangerous—stay away from him!*

She jammed her legs into unfaded jeans and pulled a red-and-white-striped top over her head before following him down to the kitchen. Just as she'd put a hand up to push open the saloon doors to the kitchen, Burke saw her.

"No, don't come in here—go sit down at the table, I'll bring breakfast out in a minute."

Miffed at his commandeering her kitchen, she sat down with her elbows on the table and her chin in her hand. But her mood lasted only long enough for him to bring her a cup of coffee.

"Here. It isn't fancy, but it'll get you going." The swinging doors swung in when he reentered the kitchen and he came right back out as they swung the other way.

Burke set an omelette down in front of her with a flourish and sat next to her, watching her eat.

"Aren't you going to have some breakfast?" she asked.

"I ate an hour ago."

Taking another bite of the delicious omelette, she wound a long string of cheddar cheese around her fork before asking, "Time enough now?"

His smile faded and he exhaled sharply, leaning back in his chair and looking intently at her. He continued, his blue eyes clouded. "When I called Southey this morning, we agreed to reactivate the Pagel project."

Her fork hit the plate with a crack. "*We* did? How nice." She got up and started for the loft. "I'll be ready to leave in half an hour," she said, her voice a low, controlled monotone.

She was seeing red when she stalked up the three steps to the loft. Loathing the petty little power games businessmen—and businesswomen—played, she'd made a point never to sign another contract with a company that played them with Pagel Associates. And now, now she'd been caught in his trap—but not for long! This was one game he was going to play alone.

Without realizing it, she'd been gripping the railing so tightly her fingers were cramping. But before she could release the rail, another hand covered hers to prevent her from going further.

"Kay! Stop a minute. I've been trying to tell you—we don't have to go back, since you brought all the reports with you. You can work on it here."

She turned and looked down into his face. She faltered for a moment as an errant impulse urged her to smooth the frown lines from his forehead; but it was gone as soon as it had formed and her eyes remained hostile.

"I can, can I? How convenient!" she spat.

His eyes darkened to opacity. "Convenient for what?" he said, challenging her.

"Stop it! I don't play power games with you or anyone. I'll finish this design back in San Diego—in my office!"

"Why can't you finish it here? Surely you can complete a simple task analysis by yourself. Or can you?"

Of course she could. But he knew it or he wouldn't have challenged her like that. And she knew how quixotic client companies could be—this wasn't the first time one of her projects had been on again, off again, though she always fought such treatment.

She opened her mouth to answer him, then snapped it shut. Suddenly she realized the business side of her brain had instinctively leaped at the chance to escape. Having to tred so carefully when she was near him was new to her, but her instincts recognized the danger even as her emotions welcomed it.

And she couldn't really blame him; he was only doing what men usually did: taking advantage of a situation. It was up to her to keep their relationship professional. But could she after last night? Her doubts put her on the defensive.

"You win," she said.

Sighing, she pulled her hand from underneath his and started walking back down the stairs. Silently she went back to the table and finished eating, though she no longer noticed the omelette's smooth, creamy texture. He'd won that round. No—she shook her head—if she started keeping a tally, this week would be unbearable.

The snapping of the saloon doors to the kitchen broke in on her thoughts and she realized Burke hadn't followed her but had gone into the kitchen instead. Pushing the empty plate from her, she was debating whether to take it into the kitchen while he was still in there, when the doors swung open again and he emerged holding a yellow sheet of paper that had been pilfered from her stack of empty legal pads.

She could tell he was watching her while he ostensibly studied the paper. His tactics lightened her mood, and she said, "It's okay, I'm not rabid."

Relaxing, he sat back down beside her and put the paper on the table in front of her. "Here's a grocery list. There isn't much left in the way of supplies, so I'd better stock up. I ran to the corner market this morning for breakfast, but we'll need more substantial fare for the rest of the week." He looked down at the table and added, "And I also need to get some clothes."

"Why don't we just go back to San Diego?" Kay asked him. "It's only a three-hour drive—barring other people's accidents. The analysis will get done just as well as here—maybe better—so why stay?"

Standing, he reached for the list and began folding it

into neat squares. "I like the place. When I was in LA, I used to come here and ski. And it isn't often I have an excuse to get away—especially when I can still call it business."

He dropped a kiss on top of her head and left, not giving her any time to react to the gesture.

On such emotional ground her footing was shaky. Kay forced herself to stand and go to the stacks of reports he had casually dumped on the window seat in the dining area. Even before she had finished reading the top page, she could feel her brain shifting gears. Soon she was gliding over the sure, confident ground of her work.

An hour later she heard the crunch of gravel from the driveway and looked up to see Burke's bright red Porsche parked there. She stood up to stretch her muscles but was interrupted by a commanding rattle of the side door.

"Quick, catch it!" Burke was standing in the doorway struggling with three grocery sacks. Kay dived forward and caught the one in front, her only thanks a mumbled "I hope you didn't break the eggs."

He dumped the remaining two sacks on the counter in the kitchen and went back outside, motioning her to go back to her work. When the sounds from the kitchen lessened, she tensed, expecting him to join her. But she was still startled when his voice drifted from behind her and his hands fell on her shoulders.

"Looks like you've made some progress out of that mess," he told her, his voice almost a caress. "I half-expected to come back and find you burning the stuff in the fireplace." His hands slid down from her shoulders to her arms as he said, "Why don't you break for lunch in about an hour?"

She nodded, not trusting her voice. Why did his touch affect her so?

His hand squeezed her shoulder. "Good," he said, and went back into the kitchen, the doors swinging back and forth. A moment later the doors opened again and she turned around to see what he wanted, but he was only stuffing some wadded-up paper into the hinges on the doors to to keep them open. He smiled at her before turning back to the counter.

Leaning over the table reading the reports made her shoulders ache and she rubbed the base of her neck to try to ease the tension. Immediately she felt two strong hands start kneading the muscles there.

His warm touch sent tremors through her and she tried to pull away. "That's okay, I'm just a bit stiff."

"Relax, Kay. I don't want you claiming disability pay because I pushed you too hard."

Disability? No, what she was feeling certainly wasn't a disability! Her pulse was much too healthy for that. He stopped after a few minutes, but the tingling sensations lasted after he had left.

Out of the corner of her eye she saw him carry in several large, awkward sacks and dump them on the bed just before he disappeared into the bathroom. The protest of the water pipes told her he was taking a shower.

Later, water was dripping onto her notes, smearing the words. "Burke," she cried, turning to look at him, then wishing she hadn't. He was standing close beside her, vigorously rubbing his wet hair with a towel. Another one was wrapped low around his waist and she had to swallow twice before she could say anything more to him.

"Burke," she said again, her voice almost cracking. "What do you think you're doing?"

"I couldn't find any scissors. Do you have any?"

"Scissors?" she asked, stupefied, watching the muscles in his chest and stomach move as he dried his hair.

"I need to cut the tags off the clothes."

"Oh, of course. I . . . I . . ." Stop. Breathe. Start over. "I think there's a pair in the stationery box on the bottom bookshelf over there," she told him, pointing to the built-in shelves along the wall opposite the fireplace. "Next to the pile of old knapsacks."

Breathing became a little easier when he walked away toward the bookshelves.

Pulling the orange-handled scissors out of the box, he waved them at her, smiling his thanks. She licked her lips and went back to her work, refusing to even think about her reaction.

"How's it coming?" he asked a few minutes later as he walked back into the room fully dressed in new jeans and a light-blue cotton knit top with dark-blue pinstriping running across it. He came and stood behind her to lean over and look at her progress, his hand resting lightly on the base of her neck.

She almost gasped aloud—his touch sent an enticing chill down her spine. Her business mind was still firmly enough in control to allow her to stand and get out of his range. "It's coming along fine, but I'll need a break soon. How about that lunch you promised me?" she said lightly as she picked up her empty coffee cup and carried it into the kitchen, her muscles protesting after being still all morning.

"I'm in charge of lunch?" he asked with deceptively mild interest, watching her from the propped-open doors.

Kay nodded as she rinsed out her cup. "You offered, didn't you?"

"I suppose I did."

"Can we eat in about half an hour?" she asked, walking passed him back to the table. Maybe if his shirts didn't fit him quite so well . . .

The sounds from the kitchen weren't all that reassuring as he banged and slammed his way around the tiny area. But Kay resolutely ignored it, trying to concentrate on her notes, though she ended up making idle marks on the paper.

A *thunk* on the end of the table interrupted her and she looked up to see Burke holding a large bulging knapsack, a smaller one resting on the table in front of him. He glanced down at her notes and smiled.

"What you need is some exercise to get the brain cells moving again. There's a great hiking trail a few miles outside of town. Let's go have a picnic by the stream."

"I suppose a break would do me some good; my muscles feel as if they haven't been moved in months!" she said, her tired cramped body overruling any second thoughts she may have had about accompanying him into the woods. "It'll only take me a minute to change," she added, heading up the stairs to the loft.

"Don't bother, you're fine," he said, "unless you have some sturdy hiking shoes to put on."

She came back down the stairs in her hiking boots and a light Windbreaker.

"Ready?" he asked, then grasped her by the elbow and propelled her toward the door without waiting for an answer.

As he was expertly guiding the Porsche over the winding mountain roads, she was starting to feel upset at having allowed him to maneuver her away from her work like this.

Breaking in on her sour reverie, he said, "I hope you like the wine; it's the same kind we had at your house."

"The wine?" she asked, then realized he was talking about that hard lump in one of the knapsacks which had been jabbing into her as she held it on her lap. "Sounds perfect." And unfortunately, it probably would be. Her teeth ground in unconscious frustration.

He turned off the main road and drove up a short paved road before coming to a parking area that proved to be the road's dead end. There were no other cars in evidence as he pulled the sleek sports car into the farthest space.

Kay hopped out and took a long, deep breath of the mountain air.

"Ah, that's lovely!" she said, twisting around to take in the view.

"The air or the view?" he asked.

"Both!" she answered, laughing, and handed over the

larger knapsack. Her spirits were beginning to revive and she watched him put on the knapsack with a graceful shrug. Hers went on with slightly less grace—her elbow caught in the shoulder strap.

"When do we start?" she asked, anxious to begin on the trail that led from a stone marker near the car out into a meadow and then into the inviting pine trees.

"If you've got your Windbreaker, we can go," he told her and headed out for the trail.

Kay ran to catch up with him, the small knapsack on her back bouncing with each step. He had stopped at the crest of the first small hill, and laughed as he watched her approach.

"I'm glad you find me so amusing," she said, hands on her hips.

Still laughing, he said, "You'd find it a lot easier going if you'd fasten the belly band."

"The what?"

"The belly band—here, I'll do it, since you've completely ignored it and let it trail down your back."

She didn't understand what he was going to do until his arms were around her. "Burke!" she cried, trying to stand back from him. But his embrace tightened and his grin widened the more she protested. Finally she gave up and stood still while he untangled the two straps she had not known what to do with and fastened them snugly around her waist.

"There," he said, not immediately letting her go, "that should be more comfortable." He dropped a kiss on her lips, but before she could react, he released her and said, "I'm famished and there's a great spot next to the stream that's not too far into the trees."

She shook her head, slightly bewildered by his mood, but took off down the trail after him.

When they reached the trees, Kay reveled in the cool shade and the crunch of pine needles underfoot; the scent surrounding them was more intoxicating than any wine.

In the distance the scatting of the stream vaguely reminded her of her favorite jazz combo.

Ten minutes later he led her out onto a shallow, grassy promontory, the water having had to bend around the unyielding land. They settled in on a thin blanket Burke had packed in the lower section of his knapsack.

Emptying the rest of the contents, Kay was surprised at the amount and variety of food—several deli salads and a large sandwich apiece. But when her hand reached the bottom of her own pack, she let out a groan.

"You brought wineglasses?" she asked.

"Only plastic ones. Why?"

"One of them broke in the bottom of my knapsack," she said, holding up the shards of plastic for him to see.

"Such fine stemware can't take all that bouncing around." He chuckled at her malevolent glance.

But once the food was before them, Kay's mood improved immediately in the crunch of lettuce and good-natured arguments over who had dibs on the last of the German potato salad. She stiffened a bit when, a few minutes into the meal, he sat down close beside her, but he smiled reassuringly.

"Don't worry, I won't eat you—I've got a sandwich to satisfy my appetite," he said with a twinkle in his azure eyes, "at least for right now."

She realized how absurd she was being and relaxed with a laugh. "It wasn't me I was worried about—I thought you wanted to steal my sandwich!"

"No, not your sandwich," he said, staring off innocently into the distance.

Kay started to react, then caught herself. *Stop it! He's going to think that's all you've got on your mind.* "And he'd be right," a tiny voice mocked.

"I don't want to steal your wineglass, either, but may I borrow it? Mine seems to have gotten broken."

A guilty flush crept into her cheeks as she stopped the

glass halfway to her lips. "Sorry, I didn't think—" she began, then was silenced by a gentle finger.

"Why don't we share it? I've had all my shots."

Laughing, she nodded her agreement and handed the glass to him. He reached out to take it, caressing her fingers as he did so. She tried in vain to ignore the fiery sensations, but when she took another bite of her sandwich, she hardly tasted it.

When they'd finished, she gathered up the trash from their feast and stuffed it into her knapsack. Burke threw the final crumpled sandwich wrapper into the sack and smiled at his minor triumph.

"I'm going to go wading," Kay said. "Want to join me?"

"Definitely not! That stream's fed by runoff from melting snow," he told her, settling under a tree.

Kay eyed the stream with second thoughts, then watched Burke as he reclined at the base of an old pine tree, looking as if he were settling in for a long winter's nap. Disgusted, she turned on her heel and walked to the sandy outcropping near a rocky bank.

The icy cold water numbed her fingers as she dangled them in the water and she reluctantly acknowledged the truth of Burke's warning. Hoping he hadn't seen her rubbing her fingers to warm them, she peeked over her shoulder at his supine figure and relaxed. His breathing was slow and even in his sleep.

She walked back toward him, watching him all the while. He had opened his shirt halfway on their walk here and now it had fallen open to reveal the taut muscles of his chest. Unbidden, the feeling of that same chest as it had felt beneath her searching fingers rose to her mind and she blushed at the tingling heat that prickled her skin. She forced herself to look away from the sight of his narrow hips and strong thighs in his snug-fitting jeans. As she looked at the random patches of wildflowers surrounding them, she tried to rein in her thoughts.

Stop it! He's a client and off limits. Sighing in self-disgust and not a little frustration, she chose a shady spot near him—not too close—and sat down. Now, if she could only convince *him* of that—and her body. When she caught her eyes wandering to his slumbering body once again, she lay down on the soft blanket and deliberately faced away from him. Her body, tired from the hike, took over and she quickly fell into a restless sleep.

Something vague and feathery fell against her cheek and she brushed it away in her sleep. Another one fell onto her and she inhaled deeply, the long breath bringing her up from the realm of sleep to consciousness. Slowly becoming aware of the hard ground beneath the blanket, she shifted her position. Suddenly another projectile landed on her and she jerked in surprise, breathing deeply again and discovering a lovely scent nearby.

Her eyes reluctantly fluttered open to discover the source of the perfume and saw a sea of wildflowers surrounding her. As she watched, another one fell among them.

Delighted, she rolled over on her back looked up at Burke. Her eyes glowed tawny with her laughter.

"Burke! I was having a perfectly marvelous dream and you had to start throwing things at me and wake me up!" Kay said, unsuccessfully trying not to smile at him. She saw no reason whatever to tell him she had been dreaming of him.

"Sounded to me as if you were planning on snoring the entire afternoon away," he said with an unrepentant grin.

The suddenness of his smile startled her. Or rather the impression it made on her senses did. A warm, gentle feeling came over her.

The knowledge dawned that his features were becoming dear to her. She was happiest when his eyes crinkled at the corners with laughter, giving him a vaguely Oriental cast. To hide the confusion her thoughts caused her, she turned away from him to gather up the flowers he had thrown and tossed them up at him in a shower of fragrance and color. "Snoring, was I?" she asked, starting to rise.

But he was faster and lay down beside her, drawing her back down with him. His hand rested lightly on her shoulder as he laughed. "Not only noisy, but violent, too! You, my sweet Kay, bear close watching."

Leaning on one elbow, she was breathless from his closeness and knew she had to move out of his range soon. That was the rational part of her brain talking, but it seemed not to be able to do more than nudge. The rest of her was thoroughly enjoying their game. It was this latter part that caused a wicked twinkle in her eyes as she dropped onto her back and freed her other arm. Immediately she reached over and began tickling his sides.

He reacted as she'd hoped he would by releasing her shoulder to protect his vulnerable sides. Then she had two hands to tickle him with and he was soon rolling over the flowers, howling with laughter.

"Kay! Stop it, Kay!" he cried between breaths, but she relentlessly pursued the sensitive skin of his sides, just above the waist.

The swiftness of his attack caught her off guard, since she had thought him helpless with laughter. But his long, agile fingers sought her sides and began to tickle her in return. Her top had somehow worked its way up and his fingers were flying over her bare skin, seeking a reaction to their feather touch.

But it wasn't the attack itself that left her stunned, but her nerves' reaction to it. She didn't feel the urge to laugh at all. The urge was for something else entirely, something she knew only Burke could give her. Whatever the rational part of her mind might have said was overwhelmed by her body's response.

His hands noticed the change in her before he appeared consciously aware of it. They subtly changed their feather touches to caresses, the sensitive fingertips drinking in her intoxicating softness. Her eyes half-closed in concentration at the exquisite sensations his fingers were calling into life, giving her a look of sensuality to which Burke reacted instinctively.

The lithe length of him moved over her, pressing along her body. She wet her lips as they parted in a sigh of pleasure at the pressure, and his own lips descended onto hers.

The moist warmth of her mouth was alive with the incendiary touch of his tongue, roaming unchallenged over the ridge of her teeth, then venturing further. Their tongues touched and sent burning messages of desire through her entire body.

In unthinking response she arched her body to his, causing a low moan to escape from deep in his throat. His hands gloried in her body, caressing, stroking, seeking out the skin that had been exposed by their earlier play. They moved under her T-shirt to her shoulders and slender back. The single clasp of her bra was undone in a moment and his hands immediately went to the full breasts freed from their confinement. In tactile wonder he explored the white globes, holding one firmly in his grasp. His mouth released Kay's only to capture one of the taut nipples with his lips, pulling and nibbling on it while his tongue teased it. An inarticulate sound of pure feminine pleasure escaped Kay at the shock of his touch.

She felt molten inside, as if the melted parts of her were flowing to the very center of her being, to the center of her womanhood, there to build up to an all-consuming release that would wrack her with its shattering electricity.

He kissed her neck in slow, sensuous progression while his hands stroked her sides and back. As he held her breasts once again, he sent electric sparks to the gathering heat in her lower body. She felt him unfasten her jeans and his hands slip inside them, caressing her hips and buttocks. The excitement his touch caused was almost unbearable and she unconsciously arched her hips toward his, feeling his want of her clearly and enticingly. Without knowing exactly how, she discovered her fingers exploring his firm-muscled back and narrow hips with insatiable strokes.

Her body demanded more and more and her hands searched lower of their own accord. Removing the rest of their clothes was the matter of only a moment and she felt him shudder when she caressed and held the firm mounds of his buttocks in her hands.

Burke's naked body was pressed onto hers, and they both continued their mutual exploration. Kay's hand roamed ever lower and drew her fingers across the back of his thighs, reveling in the feel of the developed tendons. His hands played feverish havoc with her own thighs, light strokes on the soft inner skin that led their inexorable way higher and higher.

Her hands continually searched over him in delight at the hard strength of him while he kissed her deeply, demanding that she hold back nothing. The rational voice was overcome and stilled by the tortuous ecstasy of his chest against her erect nipples and the anticipation of his upward-moving hand.

He brought his hand up in a sweeping caress to hold a breast, exciting the nipple to stand higher than before. Kay groaned with pleasure at the touch and called out even louder when he tweaked its very tip and sent such an arc of electricity through her that her hips rose up off the ground to demand fulfillment.

"Kay, my darling Kay, I want you for all time," he said, his voice rasping out of his throat.

"Burke! I want you—now!" she cried out in a thick voice.

He kissed her with an overwhelming passion and moved to cover her body with his as he fulfilled the promise his hands had made.

She cried out her joy and they were lost in each other while the rhythm of their sensual poetry carried them further into the heights of shared pleasure. Kay's entire being was centered around the furnace Burke was creating, feeling the flames lick upward.

Then the flames burst free of the restraints, overriding all of her other senses with an ecstatic power that was totally new. Her body shuddered and she heard a far-off voice cry out in incoherent wonder as Burke followed her to the summit. He shivered with an intensity that left him breathing in gasps before a low cry was wrenched from deep within him.

They lay in each other's arms for several silent moments. Only the distant whisper of the stream could be heard, a silence having descended over the area which, in their total absorption in each other, they failed to notice.

Burke shifted to lie beside her, still cradling her in his arms. He drew his index finger gently along her jawline. He appeared transfixed by her beauty, her eyes still heavy and golden with spent passion. Safe in the protective shelter of his arms, she felt the power he had over her, though she hoped he hadn't sensed how complete her capitulation had been.

Vague stirrings of discontent were disturbing the halcyon flow of her mind. As her head lay in the hollow of his shoulder, her eyes watched his chest rise and fall with his breathing. But her mind—her rational, pragmatic self—had been suppressed for too long and was returning with a vengeance.

What was she getting herself into? What *had* she gotten herself into? As the languid sense of peace and well-being faded, a feeling of discontent filled the void. Not only was Burke a client, but when Gloria and Steve had first gone to Southey, they'd come back with rumors that Huntingdon was the head of ESSCO's shock troops. That meant he'd whip Southey Manufacturing into shape and move on. By no stretch of the imagination could she think he had been permanently appointed as Southey's president.

How could she have gotten involved with such a man?

Thinking the relationship was ill fated from the beginning —it should never have even *had* a beginning—she decided she would just have to get uninvolved.

Burke had evidently felt her body tense and asked, "What's the matter, my love?" He kissed her brow to soothe the tenseness there. When she didn't answer him, he leaned back slightly to focus better on her face and said, "Is something wrong?"

A rumbled warning sounded in her brain and she pulled back from his embrace, all passion draining away into her anger at both herself and Burke for perpetuating an impossible situation. Breaking away from his encircling arm, she was starting to tell him this couldn't happen again, when he stood.

"We'd better go, honey," he said, ignoring her words. He handed her her clothes and dressed himself, all in a controlled hurry.

"Burke!" she said, angry now at his seeming disinterest. She went to gather their picnic remains. "Why won't you listen . . ." The deep throaty rumble sounded again, but this time she realized it wasn't her brain sounding a warning, but a huge black thunderhead.

"Kay, come on—don't stand there snapping at me— we've got a fifteen-minute hike ahead of us. I don't think we'll make it as it is." He picked up their hastily packed knapsacks, and throwing her the smaller of the two, started off down the trail. She hurried to scoop up her Windbreaker before following him.

It was probably this single-minded concentration that made him so good at what he did, but it was certainly difficult to deal with on a personal basis. Scurrying in his wake, she tried to observe his back objectively, but was appalled at her entirely subjective response to the movement of his strong legs and shoulders in front of her.

Though she tried to ignore it, the warmth of their encounter still filled her. How could this continue?

They were almost out of the trees when the unnatural

stillness was broken by a sudden wind blowing through the woods. It had no direction and blew first one way, then the next, leaving eddies of dead leaves and pine needles. The wind was immediately followed by a loud, insistent crash of thunder hard on the heels of a blinding flash of lightning. Burke had gotten a ten-yard lead on her, but at that, she ran to catch up. He evidently heard her quickened steps, because he also increased his pace, so soon they were both running along the trail, though Burke curiously never outdistanced her.

Just as they broke through the trees, the rain started to come down, drenching them with huge wet drops. Rain splashing in her face blinded Kay momentarily and she tripped on an exposed tree root and fell with a hardness that testified to her speed.

"Damn!" Trying hard to ignore the pain in her ankle, she got up to continue. They had to clear the crest of the small hillock before reaching the parking lot—and safety. The rain was coming down in torrents now and she was thoroughly wet. Wincing at the pain in her ankle as she tried to put her weight on it, she was almost standing when she found herself lifted off her feet and held tightly against a warm, if damp, chest.

"This isn't necessary!" she yelled above the sounds of the rain and wind.

But he didn't answer her. Hunching his body low to protect her from the storm, he ran up the hill, carrying her close to him. She could feel him straining to reach the top, trying not to lose his speed near the dangerous crest. She held her breath as they went over the top, praying lightning wouldn't strike them at that vulnerable moment.

Holding her tightly, he plummeted down the other side to the welcome haven of the Porsche.

CHAPTER FIVE

Kay watched the sheets of water assault the windshield, trying to gather the courage to thank him.

"Thank you, I—" she began, but he waved her to silence.

"It was nothing," he said, putting the keys in the ignition. "But I'm worried about getting back—I hope the roads aren't flooded out yet."

"Is it wise to leave? I'd have thought you'd want to stay until it lightened up. These cloudbursts are usually over quickly, aren't they?" She didn't relish the idea of driving through the gray nothingness outside the car.

"If we do stay, the roads *will* wash out and we'll be stuck until this is over and someone realizes we're not back yet," he said, his face grim. "And that could be a while, since no one knows we're gone."

She shivered at the idea of being stranded there. In tones as calm as she could make them, she said, "Well, we've both driven in storms before, so let's go. I can navigate for you."

The car came to life, though that was made evident more by the vibration than by any sound audible from the engine. Burke twisted his body around to see out the rear window, so as to back up the car. When they were facing the narrow road leading out to the main road, he paused. "Tell me if any cars are about to pull out," he said, then added unnecessarily, "or if I start to drive off the road."

He grinned when her eyes flashed in annoyance at his teasing.

"I can hardly see anything out there but grayness and water!" she answered, her voice a mixture of disgust at his words and uneasiness at their situation. She certainly wasn't afraid of storms, but she wasn't very fond of them, either.

"Try and settle down a bit, Kay. People have slower reaction times when they're tense and nervous."

She nodded absently at his words. Why had she ever agreed to this? Feeling the car move forward as Burke began easing the car down the road, she glanced at him in dismay.

Why had she ever met this man? She should have sent Steve and Gloria back, saying they were perfectly qualified to do the job, instead of letting her anger get the better of her and deciding to do the job herself. *Anger and something else,* a tiny voice reminded her. She quickly thrust the thought away, instinctively knowing her own motives couldn't take too much scrutiny.

"Watch closely," Burke's voice interrupted. "We're almost to the main road."

"I can't see a thing out there! It's all vague shapes that suddenly loom out at me—wait, there's the stop sign," she said, putting all of her concentration behind trying to see into the sodden gray world. "I think I see something coming—I'm not sure, it could just be a tree." Seconds later a dark, silent shape drove eerily past them and Kay shuddered. It was a car! A shiver of fear race down her spine; it had appeared to be little more than a shadow!

"Good," he said tonelessly in his concentration, "anything else? I think I'm clear on this side."

She peered hard into the gray mist, but saw no shadows. "Clear."

The next two hours, as the car crept along, were the worst Kay had ever been through. The only words that passed between them were terse questions and answers about the road, and she tried not to think of the sheer drop down the mountain to her right.

Though relaxing slightly when they turned into the valley and left the side of the mountain, she didn't sigh in relief until they'd pulled into the driveway. But the relief was replaced with dismay when she saw the pools of water that were threatening to join together and form one big lake around her cabin if the rain continued to fall. Burke drove the car as far up the driveway as he could and stopped.

"We'll have to make a run for it from here," he said, unfastening his seatbelt. "We can leave the rest of this stuff in the car until the weather clears. How's your ankle?" he added almost as an afterthought.

Unconsciously dismissing his question with a gesture, she took a deep breath and said, "It's okay. Let's go."

The roar of the storm surrounded them as they opened the car doors, the rain resoaking their clothes in seconds. Kay ran to the front door, her feet moving in a zigzagging pattern to avoid the deeper puddles and the swift stream that had formed itself through the middle of the front yard. Her ankle screamed its protest at her harsh treatment, and when she reached the relative dryness of the porch, she leaned against the door to take her weight off it.

Burke was right behind her. He bounded up the step and put an arm around her shivering frame as he reached forward and unlocked the door. Stepping drippingly into the living room, Burke tightened his hold on her, his mouth seeking hers in a hard, passionate kiss that gave her no chance to protest. Then, just as suddenly, his lips were gone and she felt herself lifted up. Her eyes widened in shock—he was taking her to the loft!

"Burke! Don't you dare!" she cried, struggling to get down. He answered only by tightening his hold on her, and she tried to reason with him. "Burke, I know you've been through a lot of tension. But don't you think . . ." she trailed off when she knew he wasn't listening.

He was getting closer to the bed and panic started to take hold of her until his steps carried them to it—and past it—and he unceremoniously set her down in front of the bathroom door. She felt like a fool.

"There. No ravishing before dinner," he said, his eyes chips of blue ice, frozen by the cold anger at her behavior. "What kind of woman are you?" He grabbed her chin, forcing her to look up at him. His eyes searched her face, and she knew that they missed nothing, from the wet channels formed by her dripping hair to golden eyes hard with a false bravado. Her mouth trembled and his thumb reached up to caress the sensitive softness. "What kind, Kay? To be a passionate, giving woman, and then, in a matter of hours, frightened of my very touch! Can you tell me, Kay? Do *you* know?"

"I'm the kind who fulfills business contracts, not false romantic dreams!" She shook her head from his grasp, hoping he hadn't seen the tears in her eyes. But she feared he had when his next words were so gently said.

"Kay, don't be afraid of what's between us," he said, stopping her retort with a light touch. "No, don't answer, just take a long, hot bath and get into some dry clothes. We can talk later."

"Damn the man!" she said under her breath as she closed the door behind her, her face wet with more than just the rain.

She brushed her dripping hair out of her face and opened the faucets full force, dumping in a handful of scented bath crystals. Stuffing an old sponge she'd found under the sink into the overflow drain, she finally turned off the water when it was just inches from the top. The water was almost too hot, but she sank into it gratefully, letting the warmth enter her chilled bones while trying to blank her mind of all thoughts.

But the thoughts wouldn't be kept back, and in a last,

desperate attempt, she let her body slide forward and completely immersed herself. Seconds later she rose to the surface, her hair dripping with the scented warm water. She brushed it back again, and propping her feet on the rim of the bathtub on either side of the faucet, leaned back to give in to her mind's insistence.

What wasn't she to be afraid of? Oh, yes, "what's between us," he'd said. But she quickly realized that trying to mock herself out of it wouldn't work. Sighing in a long breath that sent bubbles flying, she rephrased the question.

What was between them? Anything long-standing? No, she thought, shaking her head, how could there be? He was on a short-term assignment with Southey Manufacturing to put it in shape before the permanent president was appointed. And giving up her company to follow him wherever he might go next was out of the question.

Maybe there was some chemistry between them; she'd never felt this kind of attraction for anyone before. Even when they'd first met, she'd felt an unusual tug somewhere deep inside of her. Maybe it *was* chemistry—it certainly was nothing more than that!

Later, as she was drying off, a knock came on the door.

"Are you all right in there?"

"I'm fine; be out in a minute," she called back.

"Okay," he answered. "I've got some wine for you when you get out. It'll help you relax and maybe help the pain in your ankle."

She had only slightly twisted her ankle and the heat from her bath had drawn out most of the pain, but all she said was "Thanks."

The last of her bath water drained out with a noisy slurp as she vigorously dried her hair with a towel. She felt curiously lighthearted, but couldn't say why.

He was wearing only a pair of dry jeans. He held her wineglass out to her as she approached the dining-room table, but as she was about to sit down next to him, he rose and lightly grasped her elbow.

"Why don't we go into the living room? You need to relax and put that ankle up, not sit on a hard wooden chair," he said, steering her to the deep cushions on the sofa. The blankets he had used last night were piled nearby and the slight depressions from where his body had lain the night before were still there.

She sat on one end of the sofa and he put a pillow on the coffee table, then had her put her feet up. "How's that feel? You're supposed to relax, remember?" he said. He set the wine bottle on the table and made her lean back against the soft cushions. "Okay?"

Nodding, she expected him to sit down next to her, but when he remained standing, she felt an absurd kind of disappointment. She looked down at her wine, hoping he hadn't seen it in her eyes.

"I won't be long," he told her.

Something in his voice made her look up. A twinkling blue gaze met hers and his mouth curved upward in a slight grin. For a brief moment their eyes held across the few feet between them, but then he turned and walked up the stairs to the loft.

When he left the room, she felt a vague disquiet but quickly pushed it to the back of her mind. Reaching for the wine bottle, she poured herself another glass. Why was she so thirsty when everything was so wet?

Outside, the rain still fell, but now it was only a light spring shower—nothing like the intense pounding they'd experienced earlier. That thought brought memories of the afternoon and of later, when they'd stood outside the door, his arm around her sending warming sparks through her cold, wet skin.

She shook herself—she couldn't keep going on like this! She was allowing herself to be lulled into a pleasant dream; pleasant, but false. There was no way to avoid it but to keep their relationship on a strictly professional basis. Sipping the last of her wine, she poured herself yet another glass. After what had already happened, she knew it would be an uphill battle, but not impossible. She had to give it a try, or else she'd be regretting the day she'd ever heard of Southey Manufacturing.

The wine was working its magic on her nerves and she leaned her head back and closed her eyes. What was that old Fred and Ginger song? She couldn't remember its name, and trying to recall how the song went, she sleepily started to hum snatches of the melody.

"That sounds familiar," Burke said.

Her head came up and her eyes opened. She wasn't at all sure how long he had been standing there. He was still in the loft above the steps, and as he had been that morning, had only a bath towel wrapped around his waist. Having dozed off, she wasn't fully conscious yet and mused at his odd habit of making her want to run her hands over the hard muscles of his stomach and down further.... She came fully awake with a shock and spilled what little was left of her wine, her hand, as she jerked upright, knocking over the glass nestled beside her.

"That tune you were humming, do you know the name of it?" he asked her.

"No, no, I don't remember," she told him. "It just started to run through my mind."

He suggested a title and even the movie it might have come from.

"You watch Fred Astaire movies?" she asked incredulously. "I thought you'd watch, well, something else."

"John Wayne?" he laughed. "I like all the old movies, but I really enjoy musicals. They're good lighthearted fun and after a high-pressure day, I like to relax like anyone else. You should try it sometime."

He walked down the steps toward her. This time he did sit beside her, causing all sorts of problems with her circulation. She started to draw back but stopped herself. The heat from his hot shower lingered and scorched her arm, already warm from his nearness.

Valiantly trying to salvage her earlier resolution, she

said, "Fred Astaire? Sure, I used to watch all his old movies. I was madly in love with him when I was an undergraduate." She stopped abruptly, realizing where her words were leading her. "That is, I really loved his and Ginger Rogers's dance scenes. Do you remember the dance they did where she wore a dress covered in feathers? That was my favorite." She licked her lips in agitation; she was babbling but she had to do something to keep her mind off the hard male body sitting so close to her.

When she saw him looking at her curling toes, she hastily pulled them off the pillow and stood up. "Do you remember that dance when she goes like this?" she asked, arching her back. Her robe fell aside as she kicked out a long, slender leg in imitation of Ginger's completely clad manuever.

He stood up and put an arm under her back and reached around her waist with the other one. Out of the corner of her eye she'd seen his towel begin to slip. Oh, God, what was she going to do now?

He held her close to him for minute until his eyes wandered past her to the near-empty wine bottle on the table. She could feel his muscles tense as he withdrew slightly and pulled her upright. After quickly reaching down to retuck his towel, he readjusted her robe and steadied her on her feet.

"Are we having an earthquake?" she asked. "The floor keeps moving."

"No, my love, we're not," he told her. Her head had somehow found his shoulder and rested itself on it. Chuckling, he added, "You look rather, er, sleepy. Why don't you go to bed early tonight? You can have a big breakfast tomorrow morning to make up for not having any dinner tonight. How does that sound?"

All the while he'd been talking, he'd been slowly escorting her toward the loft. She nodded absently as she tried to negotiate the bottom step.

The last thing she remembered that night was the feel of his cool lips on her forehead.

The early morning sun woke her again as it slipped through the tiny uncovered space between the curtains. She snuggled closer into Burke's arms and had started to drift off to sleep again when she froze.

Burke! Her head jerked back and she found herself staring into his sleeping face. But before she could even wonder at her predicament, his eyes fluttered open and she was staring into them. Idly noticing how bright a blue his eyes were when he was at rest, she quickly pushed the thought away and tried to dwell on what could have happened last night. Surely she hadn't . . . not again!

"Good morning," he said, still drowsy with sleep. He yawned and stretched, causing Kay to admire his lithe, muscular form before she caught herself.

"Good morning," she said noncommittally. She moved to get out of bed but didn't when she realized she didn't have any clothes on. Was her memory fuzzier than she'd thought?

"What did we have for dinner last night? My mouth feels like the Prussian army marched through it," she said, trying not to look at him.

He chuckled and drew her attention. "Well, I had a nice little steak, done to a turn, with some broccoli in butter sauce, and you had a bottle of Château St. Jean Chardonnay."

"Didn't I have anything else?"

"No."

She closed her eyes tightly for a moment to block out the terrible visions of what she might have done last night. But it was only one bottle of wine, so she shouldn't have done anything too outrageous.

"Don't worry, I tucked you into bed even before I had dinner. The lampshades are all still in place." He chuckled again and she opened her eyes and turned to frown at him.

Burke was on his side, facing her, his right elbow supporting his weight. The sheet had fallen down to just below his waist and the slight muscled ridges of his taut stomach drew her to touch him, but she managed to keep her hand where it was. The golden hair on his chest formed a V that tapered down invitingly to his stomach and disappeared provocatively under the sheet. Finally she raised her eyes to his face and was startled by the tender amusement she saw there.

"Do I pass, inspector?"

A faint smile touched her lips as she nodded her assent. *Passing* wasn't how she would have described the sensually arousing body next to hers. Her smile broadened at the thought.

Her reaction put him at ease, and she watched the tenseness recede from his body. A masculine hand traced down her cheek to her jawline; then its touch was removed. Kay had to restrain her body's inclination to lean forward as if to encourage his touch. It really was too bad he was a client.

"The analysis!" She'd completely forgotten about it. How could she have allowed herself to do such a thing? Never mind that it had taken her so long to recover from Burke's "lunch" yesterday, the fact remained that it had to get done and she'd only worked on it for half a day.

Oblivious to the sight she made, she threw back the covers and quickly rose. The morning was chilly and she grabbed a light-brown pair of corduroy pants and shoved her arms into a green plaid blouse, not taking the time to put on a bra, and hastily buttoned the bottom four buttons on her way to the bathroom. She saw Burke watching her with a silly grin on his face, but by that time her mind was concentrating on her work.

Splashing some water on her face and brushing her teeth so fast she jammed the toothbrush into her gums, she walked to the kitchen in a few long strides and started some coffee. Waiting for it to perk, she popped some bread into the toaster and went back out to the dining room and sat down. Soon she had papers spread out around her, a yellow pad half-filled with notes in front of her.

She was finishing her second cup of coffee when Burke slowly walked down the loft steps and sauntered into the kitchen, pausing briefly to look in silence over her shoulder. A few minutes later he brought out a steaming cup of coffee, and sitting by the phone in the living room, dialed it and began talking.

Frowning at his actions, though not knowing why, she returned to her yellow pad and started working again. But whenever she reached a lull, she looked up at Burke, expecting him to say something or at least smile at her. But, no, he remained turned away from her, immersed in what he was saying and ignoring her completely. She was really disgusted when she reached back to rub her stiff shoulders and he didn't even look up, let alone offer to rub them for her.

Thoroughly miffed at him, she ripped her paper trying to cross a particularly recalcitrant *T*. How could he expect her to get any work done when he insisted on being so annoying!

Finally he hung up the phone and smiled at her. "How's it coming?"

She gave him a brilliant smile and said, "Fine." She turned back to her work, now suddenly finding it interesting. But twenty minutes later, when she was finishing up an important section, she idly thought what a remarkable smile Burke had—and froze.

What had she been doing? She'd been grumpy and found the work tedious all because he hadn't *smiled* at her? Trembling at the implications, she went into the kitchen and opened a Seven-Up. It took her several tries to get all the ice into the tall, narrow glass, but it wasn't until the bubbles were popping out of the top that she let her mind go back to Burke.

Why was she letting this happen to her? For three years

she'd been struggling to put Pagel Associates on its feet and today it was one of San Diego's most respected training and instructional development companies. But what had happened to the Kay Pagel who'd accomplished it against the odds?

Disgusted with herself, she forcibly put Burke from her mind and directed all her energies into the work at hand. When a thought of him tried to intrude, she would brusquely push it aside and continue working.

A couple of hours later a hand on her shoulder startled her, and she was suddenly brought back to the cabin's dining room from the abstract midst of Southey's training problem.

"Oh, Burke! I'd forgotten about . . . about lunch," she said, faltering when she'd almost had said "about you." Which wasn't entirely true; she'd just been refusing to think about him.

"Why don't we fix some lunch; you deserve a break," he said, running his hand from her neck to her shoulder.

She jumped up from her chair and said overenthusiastically, "Good idea!" and headed for the kitchen to escape his disturbing caress.

"The supermarket has a great deli," he said, rummaging around in the refrigerator. "Here's some turkey left over from yesterday, and some roast beef—rare—and here's some fruit salad we didn't have room for and a three-bean salad that wouldn't fit, either." As he mentioned each item, he put out the white paper-wrapped meats on the counter, followed by the quart containers that held the salads.

The rest of the sandwich makings followed as Kay got the plates and knives. Burke opened the fruit salad and speared a piece of watermelon with a fork, and offered it to her. She couldn't resist the watery red chunk and took it off the tines with her teeth, trying not to dribble watermelon juice down her front.

Smiling at the wonderful taste of the fresh fruit, she slid

the cutting board from its hiding place, and wielding a massive chef's knive, sliced the tomatoes before spreading mayonnaise on the slices of sourdough bread.

"There, it's ready—and none too soon. I'm starving!" Burke said, scraping the last of the bean salad onto his plate.

"You? What about me? I didn't have much of a breakfast, either, and *I've* been working!" She laughed, trying to ignore the way he made her pulse race when she stood next to him.

"Touché, my love," he said, looking out the saloon doors into the dining room. "And I don't think you'd want kidney beans all over your report, either. Where else can we eat?"

Her heart jumped at the endearment, but she didn't want to think why he made her heart react like a marionette. "There's a picnic table on the back patio, but it's probably covered in pine needles and who knows what else."

He opened the door and looked out. "You're right, but it's either that or the floor."

Ten minutes later the table was functional if not spotless. Kay brought out some paper towels to use as place mats and they sat down to eat.

"I called the office this morning," Burke told her. "They'd like to see the analysis next Monday. I told them it'd be no problem."

Kay nodded. Monday would be close, but Gloria and Steve had both done a super job and had provided her with an excellent groundwork. Then the implication of Burke's conversation hit her and she felt the blood rush from her face. Everyone knew they were here together!

"Kay! What's wrong? You're white!" He started to get up and come around the table to her. "It couldn't be food poisoning so fast, could it?"

"NO! No. I'm fine," she said, finding her voice. "I just thought of something I'd meant to do and didn't." She put her sandwich down and looked at her plate. A large round lump had taken up residence in her stomach. When word of this got around . . . It would take her years to make up for the damage that would have been done. And what about the other women in her company? Kay knew how hard it was to take the sly innuendoes and suggestions when there *wasn't* anything behind them. But now?

She was close to being physically ill when Burke broke in on her thoughts.

"Kay, why won't you tell me what's wrong?"

Looking up, she saw the concern clouding his eyes and shook her head. No, she couldn't blame him; it was her own fault for not insisting they leave when the project was back on. "I've just realized how major a blunder I've made by staying up here with you. Not only will Pagel Associates suffer, but the women who work for me will be the victims of all sorts of propositions. How could I do that to *them?*"

"Blunder? How so? No one knows we're here together," Burke said, frowning deeply. His brows almost met over his nose as he looked at her. "Ticher and his crew only know I'm up here on a spur-of-the-moment vacation. They also know you happen to be in the same vicinity. In fact, I told them I'd be sure and stop by and let you know the new deadline."

"Burke, it's too risky," Kay said, shaking her head. She relaxed at his words, glad to know the damage hadn't been done *yet*—now it was up to her to make sure it didn't happen at all. "We've got to go back."

"For God's sake, Kay, no one expects you to live like a hermit!" he said, his eyes showing his disappointment at her cowardice. He stood and leaned on the table, his face close to hers as it once had been over a conference table at Southey.

Exasperated at her, he said, "Kay, your work is *here;* that analysis has to get done. And be honest, with yourself at least—could you get it finished by Monday if you were in your office, with everyone badgering you with trivial decisions they're too afraid to make themselves?"

She had to admit it would be rough to get it out by Monday at her office, but she also had plenty of distractions here—the major one of which was now hovering over her. But maybe she was blowing it out of proportion. How many people ever concerned themselves over Kay Pagel's private life?

"Why do I always find myself giving in to you?" she asked. The color had returned to her face and the lump in her stomach wasn't quite so noticeable, but the constraint of her fear was still in the air between them.

"You've got a lot of good sense." He lowered himself back down to his seat, though the muscles along his shoulders didn't relax and his eyes lost only part of their chill.

After lunch Burke cleaned off the table and quickly washed the dishes while Kay went back to work. As she bent over her notes, she missed his touch more than ever. She refused to acknowledge how much she wanted him to walk over and rub the stiffness out of her shoulders again.

Several times during that afternoon she looked up and saw him watching her with his mouth turned down in a small frown.

The tenseness of the afternoon took its toll on Kay's muscles, as she discovered when she tried to rise after sitting stiffly for hours.

"Ohhhh, I hurt everywhere," she said to the room at large. Her hands over her head, she arched backward, then swung her arms down to touch her toes. Her joints popping loudly, she raised herself up and did several more exercises. When she looked up, Burke was leaning against the back of the sofa, his arms crossed over his chest and his long legs stretched out in front of him. He was smiling as he watched her efforts.

She smiled back with an impish grin that froze when she remembered she'd never buttoned the top three buttons of her blouse. Her hands started to move toward her neckline, but she controlled them. He would only laugh at her being so self-conscious.

"What do you say to dinner and some dancing? There's a great place near the lake," he said, his eyes never leaving her.

She looked at him silently, his muscular thighs giving her some idea of what dancing with him would be like. At the thought of moving slowly to a primal rhythm with him on a dance floor, a delicious tremor ran through her. She had to bite her lip to get her mind back on track; she must be more tired than she had thought.

She started to shake her head no, but her words were out before she realized what she was saying. "Sure! Just let me go up and change."

A quick shower helped her slough off some of her tiredness, but even before she had fastened the lovely rose dress that was the only dress she'd brought with her, her tiredness returned. She finished putting on her high-heeled shoes and sat on the edge of the bed for a moment, staring off into the distance.

A few minutes later Burke came up the stairs and found her there. Chuckling, he pulled her to her feet and held her close to him, his hands running down her back over the snug-fitting Qiana of her dress.

"I think I'll take a rain check on the dancing," he said in a low, caressing voice as he led her around the end of the bed.

"I'm sorry, Burke. I don't know why I'm so tired," she said, yawning.

"I don't know, either, unless it's because you've worked almost straight through for the past twelve hours," he observed dryly. "I can fix you some dinner if you're hungry."

"Thanks, but I think I'll just go to bed." He leaned down to kiss her good-night, but she bent over to unfasten her shoes in time to avoid the searing heat of his lips.

As she slipped between the sheets, the last thing she heard was a subdued clatter from the kitchen.

She woke with a start. She'd been dancing with Burke in an elegant restaurant and she'd started to . . . what? Opening her eyes had little effect in the darkness and it took them a while to adjust to the faint moonlight filtering through the curtains. Looking across the large, king-sized bed, she saw Burke's long form on the other side. Her hand started to reach out to touch him, but she caught herself.

She remembered now. In her dream she'd been reaching for him. But why had she awakened?

The mountain nights were unpredictable and this night was chillier than the others had been. She'd worn a nightgown to bed, but a faint shiver ran down her spine. Carefully getting out of bed, she walked over to the closet and tried to search for her robe by the moon's luminescence. She couldn't locate it, but found a warm sweater that would work just as well. Putting on a pair of lamb's wool slippers, she lightly walked down the steps to the living room, her slippers making a barely audible swishing sound on the wood.

The silence of the night pressed around her, reinforced by Burke's regular breathing and her own ragged breaths. Quickly going through the kitchen, she opened the back door and went out onto the patio.

She walked into the moonlight, her sweater wrapped tightly around her. The patio was as she and Burke had left it that afternoon, and she sat down at the picnic table where she had before. Out there under the lonely stars struggling to shine through the trees, she felt alone.

In her mind's eye he loomed over her again as he had that afternoon, his eyes the color of the sky on an arctic morning.

Playing idly with a pile of pine needles that had blown onto the bench beside her, she recalled what she'd felt then

. . . and later, when he'd been watching her exercise and his long, muscular legs were stretched out in front of him. Why did she keep having to push away her thoughts of him? Because when she thought of him, she thought of yesterday afternoon by the stream. She thought of the touch of his skin under her hands, the taut muscles that rippled across his shoulders as he moved, and she thought of those hard, powerful legs and how they had felt pressed against her smoothness.

Leaning her head back to drink in the cool mountain air, she knew she also thought of her desire. For him, for Burke Huntingdon, and all that he had demonstrated her body was capable of feeling.

She desired him. And *that* is what had brought her out of her dream. She'd been reaching for him to draw him down to her on the dance floor in her dream, down to meet her and take her to the heights he had shown her. But even in her dreams she hadn't been able to admit it to herself. Why could the night air make her more truthful than her own subconscious?

She heard the back door open and she quickly stood, facing Burke as he came out to meet her. Her emotions weren't ready to meet him yet, the revelations too new for her to understand how to file them away.

He came silently and stopped in front of her, and then his hands went inside her sweater to grip her shoulders through the thin material of her gown.

She reacted by instinct. In the moonlight she had let her guard down and he hadn't given her enough warning for it to reappear. Her head tilted back and her eyes half-closed as she offered her lips up for him to kiss. His hands traveled down, lingering on the mounds of her breasts before continuing on to her waist. He pulled her to him and his hands traveled back up as he crushed her to him in a kiss that overwhelmed her senses.

Left free of direction, she opened her teeth to admit his questing tongue, and explored his own moist, warm mouth. Her tongue danced over his teeth to the slick inner surfaces of his cheeks and she could taste the tannin from the wine he'd evidently had at dinner. The friction caused by the rough surfaces of their tongues as they met and slid across one another sparked a greater response from her body and she shivered.

But something of what had forced her out of her dream remained and she abruptly brought the kiss to a close. She turned away from him and sat back down on the picnic bench, her head buried in her arms, confusion over her feelings keeping her silent.

He sat down beside her and started to massage her neck with one hand. Her traitorous body responded immediately to his closeness, and she leaned over and relaxed in the comfort of his arms. His arm dropped from her shoulders to encircle her waist and he pulled her even closer into his protective hold.

"Burke," she began, but found his fingertips on her lips.

"Shhh," he said quietly, "it isn't the time to think or say anything."

She nodded sleepily, having trouble keeping her eyelids open. Her head was feeling heavy and finally she gave in and rested it against his shoulder. Gently he led her back into the house to sleep.

CHAPTER SIX

Burke wasn't anywhere in sight the next morning, but the Porsche was in the driveway. Kay made some coffee and went to work after deciding to postpone breakfast, resolutely ignoring her growling stomach.

After an hour the report was flowing along rapidly and she estimated she could get it done early tomorrow if the pace kept up. Bending back over her work, she had started on the next paragraph; then she heard the side door open and looked up.

He wore a plaid flannel jacket to ward off the chill of the crisp mountain spring morning and a pair of dark-blue jeans. Kay watched him as he removed the jacket, revealing the light-blue turtleneck sweater that fit him so very well. With his eyes glowing a bright sapphire blue and his cheeks slightly pink from the chilly morning air, she felt her heart stir at the handsome sight he made.

"Had breakfast yet?" he asked, coming to stand in front of her as she rose. He reached up and tucked a fallen curl back behind her ear, the intimate gesture appearing natural to him; but she stepped back. To cover the movement she picked up the last report she'd been working on.

"No, but I'm starving!"

His grin made her pulse flutter in her throat. "Good. It'll be ready in five minutes flat." He glanced down at her mug of coffee amid the piles of papers. "Make that four and a half minutes if you've already made the coffee."

About ten minutes later the timer in the kitchen went

off. Burke appeared with a tray of delicious-looking pastries, warm from the oven and covered with melted butter. She half-turned her chair toward him, crossing her long legs as if to emphasize her next words.

"Those look wonderful, but I can't eat them!" Kay cried. Naturally he set the plate down directly in front of her, casually pushing her notes out of the way.

"Why not?" he asked, his eyes traveling down her, from the green-and-gold print blouse to her forest-green corduroy pants to her feet clad only in fuzzy brown socks. "You can always exercise." When his eyes returned to her face, there was a distinct twinkle in them.

Her hand unconsciously went to her blouse, and then she felt foolish—she'd remembered to button *this* one up all the way, though it had a lower neckline than she'd have liked.

He smiled at her gesture and she quickly lowered her hand and reached for a pastry in one movement. They did look good and she hadn't had much to eat yesterday, she rationalized.

Biting into one, she closed her eyes to savor the sinfully rich taste. Unexpectedly she felt Burke's warm lips caress her skin just below her jawline, sending a fiery message through her veins. His tongue teased at the corner of her mouth. She swallowed hard and bent back before giving in to her impulse to return his kiss.

"I didn't have any napkins," he said.

Puzzled at his words, she stopped her retort and looked at him quizzically.

"The butter started dribbling down your chin," he said with a warm smile, "and I didn't have any napkins."

She had started to take another bite, but put the pastry back on the plate instead. Giving him a long considering look, she turned and went into the kitchen, returning with an entire package of napkins.

"There," she said with a smug smile as she picked up her pastry again with a napkin under it.

"Chefs have to get some reward," he said, pulling out a chair and sitting next to her. "Not that I recall signing on as a chef."

"I don't recall your signing on as *anything*. Stowed away is more like it."

"Stowaways don't usually navigate the ship."

"You didn't have to stay, Burke," she said. "Why did you?"

It was his turn to look uncomfortable and he only shrugged and said, "It's not often company presidents run away from me. Maybe I just wanted to make sure you understood you didn't have to."

His words were unsettling, implying more than she wanted him to. Kay shook her head; it was nonsense to dwell on it. Whatever kind of relationship he might want was out of the question.

She finished her bear claw and he took the pastry plate into the kitchen and returned with two fresh mugs of coffee. "I've got some phone calls to make, so I'll let you get back to work."

It took her some time before she could recapture her earlier pace, but soon she was involved in the task analysis for Southey Manufacturing. Involved until three hours later, when Burke slammed the phone down with an oath.

"Where is that man! He should at least have checked in with his secretary by now," he said, standing up and almost knocking over the sofa in his agitation. The phone rang and he ripped off the receiver and shouted, "Hello!"

"Edwin! You're a hard man to locate," Burke said, sitting back down on the sofa. Kay assumed Edwin was the lost man and turned back to her work.

The sun had been fighting bravely against the onslaught of the gray clouds and was finally victorious. It was nearing noon when its bright shafts of light flowed through the dining-room window and across the table to her work. She smiled at the patch of welcome sun and stretched backward, folding her arms behind her head.

Burke came up behind her and put his hands on her shoulders, the warmth from his touch rivaling the sun's. "We can't waste this sunshine on a task analysis! How about trying grass skiing?"

"Grass skiing? When there's a lake close by to go fishing? Never!" Kay laughed. "But as much as I'd love to, I really can't take the time."

"Ice skating? I think there's a rink up here."

She shook her head. "Thanks, Burke, but I've got to get this done." Swiveling in her chair, she turned and looked up at him. "Don't I?"

The smile on his face made him look like a small boy with a marvelous scheme. "You've got until next Monday, and you said you could probably get it done tomorrow. Plenty of time to go horseback riding."

Her eyes narrowed and she watched him closely. "Why don't you want to go fishing?"

He removed the hand that had been resting on her shoulder and sat down next to her. Leaning back in his chair, he stretched his legs out in front him, crossing them at the ankles. With half-closed eyes he watched her as he shrugged. "No reason."

"Burke, have you ever been fishing?"

He was silent so long she didn't think he was going to answer her.

"No."

"What, never?"

He threw his head back and laughed before answering her with a full-bodied baritone rendition of "Har-r-r-d-l-l-y ev-ahhhhh!"

Laughing in return, Kay told him, "Okay, Captain Corcoran, you're about to give up the HMS *Pinafore* for a real live boat!" She stood up to emphasize her decision, and instinctively put out a hand toward him. Wanting immediately to draw it back, she told herself she couldn't be so cowardly and held it out firmly.

He grasped it as he stood up, drawing it up over his

shoulder to allow him to put his hands around her waist. "All right, mate, I'll let you initiate me into this barbarous ritual." One of his hands traced a sensuous, possessive trail down her side, the heel of his hand going over the mound of her breast, completing its journey on the swell of her hip.

"Trout. The lake's stocked with trout, so we could get lucky," she said breathlessly. Many more caresses like that one, and she'd be dragging him, but it wouldn't be to the lake.

Disgusted with herself for blushing at the thought, she escaped from his hold as he gave another shout of laughter.

"And bass, too, no doubt!" He stood there grinning after her as she ran up to the loft to get her shoes.

Grabbing a sweater to pull on over her blouse, she met him back downstairs. After a quick lunch at a small café they stopped at a drugstore and picked up a few items before driving down to the marina. They chose a small boat with an outboard motor and Kay took them to the far side of the lake before shutting off the power. A slight breeze disturbed the water just enough to rock the boat gently.

She tilted her head back to drink in the sunshine. "It's turned into a beautiful day!"

"So why ruin it for a poor blameless fish?" he asked.

There were three bench seats in the boat and Kay sat on the one near the bow and Burke faced her on the center one. She grinned at him, but reached down and picked up one of the fishing rods they'd rented. Leaning forward, she showed him how to put it together and how to control the spinning reel.

He put his thumb near the bail and held the rod upright, the sinkers and dangerous hooks swinging at eye level. Cautiously bending backward to avoid getting her ears pierced for a second time, she maneuvered so she was sitting next to him. Reaching around to his other side, she grasped his hand. "I think you'd better tilt it out toward the water more."

"Spoilsport. Fish aren't the only thing I could catch on a sunny afternoon," he said, but he dutifully dangled the lethal end over the water with one hand while the other encircled her waist. The end plopped into the water as he released the bail; she shook her head.

"No, you can't release it so soon," she told him, then leaned forward to show him how. "Here, like this." But as she reeled the line back in, she realized he was watching her face rather than her actions. She swallowed hard and tried not to look at him, but his intensity was disconcerting.

"Beautiful," he whispered.

A plop told her she'd released it much too soon herself, but she wasn't concentrating on the reel anymore. In fact it was hard to focus on anything at all, when her senses were being overpowered by the heat from his body and his masculine scent was drugging her.

She started to take a deep breath and stopped as his tantalizing mixture of his soap and aftershave and sheer maleness made her head spin like the fishing rod's reel. "Here, this way. You should do it this way," she told him, bringing all her control to bear.

When he finally started to get the hang of it, she judiciously edged away from him and said, "You don't really have to go through all this, since we can just drop the lines over the side." She couldn't help giggling at the thundering look he gave her.

An hour passed as they dangled their lines in the water, but they only caught trout too small to keep. Throwing the last one back, Burke reeled in his line and put the fishing rod in the bottom of the boat.

He pushed up the sleeves of his turtleneck and then sat looking at her, his elbows resting on his knees.

Her line started to bob up and down, and flashing him

a confident grin, she started to reel in her catch. When it turned out to be another tiny one, Burke returned her grin.

"Want me to return him to the bosom of his family?"

Nodding, she watched him carefully remove it and throw it back into the water. "If that's all the better I can do, I think I'll give it up, too." Shading her eyes as she looked up toward the sun, she added, "I'm getting hot."

Storing her fishing rod next to his, she started to pull off her sweater. When it was halfway off, she realized her blouse was coming off with it and stopped. The sweater covered her mouth, and only her nose and eyes peeked out over the neckline.

Peering out at him as he sat there watching her with an amused grin splitting his face, Kay tried to maneuver her arms out of the sleeves but she couldn't get her elbows to cooperate.

Before she could stop struggling, Burke had slid his hands up her sides to grasp her blouse and had tugged it down. "Okay, try it again," he said, holding the blouse firmly.

His hands were high on her sides, his thumbs resting just under her breasts. The heat from his touch branded her sides, sending a wave of anticipation through her, and she stopped struggling immediately. She waited, trance-like, for his hands to move across her skin with the slight friction that was as a bellows to her flame. But his hands didn't move and her face disappeared beneath the sweater as she slowly removed it.

His hands held her for a moment after she lowered her arms, his thumbs exploring the gentle swell of her breasts at the sides. Sensing his breathing quicken, Kay heard her own sharp inhalation. She raised a shaking hand to brush back her mussed hair, the strands almost gold in the sunlight, and he dropped his hands at last.

"Would you mind if I took off my sweater, too? It *is* getting hot," he observed, looking out across the water to the nearby solar observatory jutting out into the lake, the muscles near his jaw moving under his skin. When she said no, shaking her head, he pulled off his own sweater but—unlike Kay—he had nothing on underneath.

"Ah, that feels good."

Next to him in the small boat Kay straightened her blouse with great care to cover her own unsettling reactions to the expanse of his bare chest so close to her, its blond hair glinting with a pale sheen.

Smiling at her, he asked, "How about something to drink?" Resting one hand on the exposed bench between them, he leaned slightly toward her.

Quickly bending down to open the ice chest, she quickly pulled out a carton of lemonade and held it between them. "Lemonade?"

He smiled at the maneuver but leaned back and nodded his head. "Not exactly what I had in mind, but it'll do for now." After drinking deeply from the glass she'd handed him, he licked his lips and rattled the ice. His smiled widened as he looked at her again.

"Better get out that suntan lotion," he told her, reaching up to tweak her nose. "You'll be sunburned before you know it."

Rummaging around in the sack, she pulled out the white-and-orange bottle of coconut oil and was tilting it to squirt some on her hand when he pulled it from her grasp.

"Here, let me do that."

"No, no, that's all right, I can do it."

"Of course you can, but I *want* to."

"Burke, I—" She stopped on a quick intake of breath. His hand, covered with the slick oil, had started sliding up and down her arm and the tiny pulses of energy his fingers sent through her skin demanded attention. Stroking upward toward her shoulder, his hand stopped only when the short sleeve of her blouse interfered. His fingers encircled her upper arm in a light grasp and his hand slowly slid back down again, hesitating over the bend in her elbow. His thumbs were careful to work in the oil with slow circular motions.

Both his hands slid up and down her arm, encasing it in the almost frictionless heat of the oil. His fingers took special care on the outside of her elbow, gently playing around the joint, making her blood pound through her veins as his hands blazed a trail across the slickened surface of her skin.

His fingers reached the apex of their journey and, unconsciously, her head bent back and she closed her eyes, luxuriating in the feel of his hand lightly tracing the inside of her arm near her body. Somewhere in her brain, alarm bells started to ring, but she ignored them and drank in the heat that had nothing to do with the rays from the afternoon sun.

Burke removed his fingers and she looked at him in confusion at the sudden withdrawal of his touch. An enigmatic smile played around his thin lips as she watched him pour more oil into his glistening palm.

She sighed as his hands reached toward her other arm, and his incendiary touch resumed its fiery travel. Her eyes closed once more when he finished with her arm and traced a finger shining with oil across the skin at her blouse's neckline. He flattened his palm against the firm, pounding pulsebeat at her throat and rubbed up and down with slight strokes, his fingers feathering the edges of her jaw.

With no warning his hand descended to the deep V of her neckline and lightly teased the swell of her breasts before returning to her neck and shoulders. Using both of his hands, he held her head and stroked her jawline.

He skimmed the hollows of her cheeks with the protective film of oil, and his thumbs caressed her cheekbones for long moments before gently tracing the tender area under her eyes.

Finishing with her temples and her forehead, he withdrew his touch. A heartbeat passed and she felt her lips being teased with a whisper of a kiss.

Slowly opening her eyes, she was temporarily dazzled by the sun shining off the water and instinctively her hand went up to shield them. It had taken her several seconds to realize he had finished, and when she looked at him, she saw he was holding the bottle of suntan oil out to her.

"Now it's your turn," he said, the odd smile still hovering around his lips.

Her eyes widened in surprise as she understood: she was to spread the oil on him, across that wide, muscular chest and down his arms.

Dared she touch him? He had lit a fire deep within her, a fire such as she had never known except when she was with him. If she continued what he had started, would she fan the heat into a burning only he could quench?

As he tilted his head to look at her, she saw a challenge twinkling deep in his eyes. Adjusting her balance to keep from leaning too far toward him in the lightly bobbing boat, she silently accepted his challenge. With a martial gleam in her eye she poured the oil into her palm and aimed for the middle of his hard chest.

Her hand missed its aim and slid over the smooth skin of his shoulder. She started rubbing fiercely in quick circles, trying to ignore the feel of his muscles.

"Not so hard!" he cried, grabbing the sides of the bench to keep her from pushing him backward.

Slowing her hand, she looked up into his face and swallowed the lump in her throat. His blue gaze held her golden one and she felt he could see into her mind and to her heart. She broke the bond and let her eyes follow her hand as it moved along the hills and hollows of his muscular torso.

The undulation of her hand over his sun-warmed skin was fascinating and her eyes took on an unfocused softness as she lost herself in the feel of him. After stopping to get more oil, she reached across to his other shoulder and down to his chest. Out of the corner of her eye she saw him watching her face, but she was too absorbed in her task to consider what it might mean.

The change from smoothness to the silky roughness of his chest hair sent her blood racing. As the fine strands bent at her touch, her veins began pulsing with their own insistent rhythm. Glorying in the tiny curls that grasped at her fingers as she buried them deep to put the protective oil on his skin, she unknowingly curved her lips upward in the same enigmatic smile Burke had worn earlier.

Her hand dipped even further, following the V of hair down to the waist of his pants. The faint ridges of his taut stomach muscles tantalized her sensitive fingertips. Reoiling her hand once again, she looked up at his face and saw his eyes still watching her intently.

"Do you want to turn around so I can do your back?" she asked softly. It was hard to think of words when her rational mind had submerged unnoticed beneath the sea of her emotions; her smile was uncharacteristically shy. Enveloped by the warmth from the sun and her own heated pulse and mesmerized by the bright pinpoints of sparkling light from the water, she was reluctant to break the spell that held her.

Wordlessly he swiveled on the bench so that his back faced her. A faint pinkish tinge covered it and she slathered the oil with both of her hands over the wide, firm expanse near his shoulders down to the smooth, narrow small of his back. Dabbing some on his neck, she let his blond hair run over her fingertips. Her hands glided up his sides one last time to make sure she had covered all of him and to revel in the sensuous feel of his skin sliding under her fingers.

"I think I've covered everything but your face," she told him. His head bent forward and she could see his back expand and contract as he took several deep breaths before raising his head again and swinging his leg back over the bench to face forward.

"Thanks, Kay." There was an almost imperceptible waver in his voice but his eyes told her nothing as he held out his hand to her. "I can do my face; I don't want your arms to get tired."

Unaccountably bereft, she silently watched him rubbing the suntan oil vigorously into his face. When he was done, the mood between them subtly altered.

Catching her eye, Burke glanced down at the fishing poles and said, "Want to try your hand again? We might get lucky this time."

"Luck has nothing to do with it," she said, smiling easily at him. "My father always maintained that a consummate amount of skill was needed, never luck!"

Fifteen minutes later Kay saw Burke's pole dip. Flashing a grin at her, he started reeling in his line. On the end, swinging free in the air, was a good-sized trout and he quickly put it in a bucket of water.

"All right, maybe a little bit of luck," she conceded.

"Luck had nothing to do with it." He leaned back and threw his line into the water again, his skin glistening as he moved.

The only sound for the next two hours was the gentle lapping of water against the side of the boat as it rocked, its soothing motion making them drowsy.

The loud roar of an outboard speeding passed startled Kay out of her half-conscious state and she straightened up, only to have to grab the side of the boat when it started rocking violently from the large swells the passing boat churned up.

"Okay?" Burke asked, once the other boat had passed.

She nodded and leaned over the side to retrieve her cork-wrapped fishing pole from the water. "Think we'd better start back? Looks like it's getting late." The sun was resting in a notch between two peaks and would soon be going down.

"Good idea. I'll go start the motor," he said, standing

up, only to sit back down quickly when the boat started its violent rocking again.

"Careful! You'll swamp us!"

He sent her a disgusted glance, then swiveled on the bench as he'd done earlier and swiftly changed from the middle to the back bench. Sitting sideways, he grasped the short starter rope and yanked. The motion threw his body against the side of the boat and set it to rocking precariously. Water lapped over the sides and the bucket of fish wobbled alarmingly.

"Burke! What are you doing?" she cried, turning around to see for herself.

Without answering her, he tried it again with the same results, only this time the bucket fell over, spilling the dead fish over Kay's feet.

"*Burke!*"

He finally turned around as she set the bucket upright and began picking up the fish by their tails. Seeing she had his attention, Kay said, "You start it like a lawn mower!" She gestured, trying to show him how to do it, but realized she still had a fish in her hand. Disgustedly throwing it into the bucket, she sighed. "Here, let me do it."

"It can't be that hard to start a damn outboard!"

She moved to join him at the stern, but the boat tilted dangerously and she stopped. "Would you please move back up here first?"

He acquiesced and moved back up beside her. As he slid down on the bench next to her, his bare chest gleamed in the last rays of the sunlight. A flutter ran through her lower stomach at the sight and she knew the fire deep inside her was far from out. But she pushed the thought from her mind and moved away from him toward the back of the boat.

The motor started with one swift jerk of the rope. Refraining from giving him a triumphant grin, she kept her face impassive as she aimed them back toward the marina.

She lifted her face to feel the wind whip past her, sleek-

112

ing her hair against her head with its force. A tiny twinge of regret went through her as she watched Burke put his sweater back on. It was indeed getting chilly now that the sun had gone behind the mountains, but she admitted the sight of him could make her tremble; a delicious warm trembling she was starting to crave.

On the drive home a feeling of happiness enveloped her and she shook out her hair in mute exaltation. Stretching her longs legs out in front of her in the car, she leaned back in the seat and smiled.

"You certainly look as if you enjoyed the trip," he said.

"Wasn't it wonderful? I *did* enjoy myself! Even if you gave our fish away," she said, laughing at the sight he'd made trying to convince a skeptical little boy who'd been fishing with his father but hadn't caught anything that it was quite all right to accept such a gift. The boy's father had stood nearby, chuckling at the scene.

"I couldn't let the poor little fellow go home empty-handed, could I?"

"But now *we're* going home empty-handed! And I'm starving!"

"What, again?"

The windows were rolled down and the fresh mountain air blew past them, invigorating and clean. Kay took a deep breath and exhaled slowly. "Ahhh, that air is wonderful. I wish we could bottle it and take—someone's barbecueing! Can you smell it?" Taking another deep breath to savor the delicious smell, she broke it off with a fit of laughter at the sound of her stomach growling with appreciation.

"Now, why do I have this odd notion you're going to ask me to stop and get us a couple of steaks?" he said, catching her starting to speak again.

"Could we? That smell is driving me crazy!" she said, smiling broadly when he pulled the car into the parking lot of the grocery store.

They arrived at the house with two full grocery sacks.

"At least we like the same barbecue sauce," Kay said, throwing the words over her shoulder as she carried in one of the bags. Putting it down on the kitchen counter, she glanced out the back door to the patio and groaned. "Burke, the grill!"

"What about the grill?" he asked as he sat his sack down next to hers on the counter.

"It hasn't been cleaned in ages," Kay said with despair in her voice. Her eyes followed Burke's hands as he took the steaks out of the sack. The look she gave them held such longing that Burke burst out laughing.

"Don't look so forlorn," he said. "We can clean it off. Put this stuff in the refrigerator and I'll get the scouring pads."

They turned on the patio light, pushed up their sleeves, and set to work. A half hour later, dirty gray foam covered their arms up to their elbows and their clothes had patches of it all over.

"Ugh," Kay said as she stepped back from the dismantled grill and looked down at herself. "I'm filthy!"

Hosing off the last of the foam from the grill, Burke nodded his agreement. "You certainly are," he said matter-of-factly. Leaning the rinsed pieces against the table's benches to dry, he turned to scrutinize her. "In fact, I'd say you're the dirtiest I've ever seen you."

"You're not in such a state of cleanliness yourself, you know. Those jeans *used* to be blue."

"Too true," he said, smiling, "but I'm too hungry to clean up. Let's rinse off the worst of it and start dinner."

She nodded and picked up the pile of discarded paper towels.

Bending over the sink, intent on keeping the dirty gray foam off the fixtures, she didn't feel him come up next to her until he was close at her side. He had rinsed off some of the foam with the hose and was much cleaner than she was.

Burke reached over and turned on the hot water.

"There," he said with satisfaction. "You can't get clean with cold water."

The enticing smell of him that she remembered so well lulled her into a fascinating world where he would always hold her close. Shaking her head to deny her attraction to him, she was brought back to reality with a painful start.

"That's too hot!" she cried. "I need clean hands, not sterilized ones!"

"Lightweight," he said with a grin as he moderated the temperature.

"That's better," she said, reaching for the soap. But he was there before her and started lathering first. Kay's frown was ignored.

He stood very close to her, so that their legs were almost touching. She watched him rub the soap up his arms, his muscles rippling with the motion. When he leaned over to rinse off the lather, the movement communicated itself to Kay's body. The long length of his thigh stretched with his action, sending a shock wave along her nervous system. She gasped at the effect.

"Here, let me do it, since you seem content to just stand there," he said lightly, grasping her hands in his strong grip.

"Burke, no!" She tried to pull away, but the slow, sensuous motion of his hands spreading the slick soap over her skin started a new ball of warmth growing inside of her and she stopped struggling. He cleaned each finger with deliberate care, and Kay thought she'd expire from the sensations he was causing as he slowly traced the inside of her fingers.

"Burke?" she murmured, the pleading note in her voice appalling her. She was once again under his spell, as she'd been that afternoon, and she felt herself sinking in the pool of sensuality he was creating.

The startling splash of water on her hands made her open her eyes in surprise. Rationality started to emerge once again, sloughing off the pull of desire.

115

"Burke!" she said for the third time, but she was calmer now.

"Here's a towel," he said, throwing one to her. "I'll go start the charcoal going."

Grabbing an old full-length apron from a bottom drawer, he was out onto the patio in a few long strides. "We still need to clean off the table," he called back to her.

Sighing both at his actions and at her own feeling of falling short of promised happiness, she swept back her hair with an impatient hand and set about unwrapping a new package of paper towels. With a sponge and the cleaner in one hand, and the towels in the other, she took a deep breath for courage and went to join him on the patio.

He was reassembling the grill when she walked out, and he gave her only a glance as she began cleaning off the table. The wind and the morning drizzle had dumped more leaves and pine needles on it.

Her unruly eyes kept wandering to watch him bending over the grill, his attention concentrated on the bright orange flame that licked up into the cool evening air. The patio light was behind him and his straight nose and prominent jaw were sharply outlined. As if sensing her eyes on him, he turned and flashed her a smile.

"It'll be a while yet before the coals are ready. Think you can hang on?" He walked over and sat down next to her.

Disturbed by his closeness, she gathered the cleaning remnants and started to rise, but his hand shot out and enclosed her wrist in a firm, light grasp.

"I don't bite," he said.

"Don't be silly, I'm not running away from you," she said, grimacing at the high, squeaky sound of her voice; but she sat back down.

His thumb was slowly rubbing the pulse spot on her wrist and she took a ragged breath. Pulling her hand away, she scooped up the pile in front of her and twirled around on the bench, away from him.

"I'll get the food," she threw over her shoulder as she escaped into the kitchen.

Quickly tossing the used paper towels in the trash, she leaned her back against the corner. "Whew!" Breathing steadily to calm her erratic pulse, she rested her hand unconsciously on her chest. "The man is good. The man is damn good. But you've *got* to get some kind of hold on yourself. This can't go on!" she whispered to the tiny room.

The cold blast from the refrigerator helped her rattled nerves to quiet down and she felt she had herself under control again. With one last deep breath she went back out to the patio with the steaks, potatoes, and corn.

CHAPTER SEVEN

An hour later the remains of their meal were scattered in front of them. It had been as delicious as the fragrance on the drive home had promised, and Kay pushed her plate away with satisfaction.

As the night advanced, the chill in the air increased and Kay inched closer to Burke's warmth without knowing she was doing so. Amid the easy camaraderie of their conversation, her resolve slipped away unnoticed.

Earlier they had turned off the patio light and now sat on the bench and watched the coals of the fire glow in the darkness. The wine had warmed her considerably, but when Burke's arm encircled her to pull her closer to him, she let the excuse of the cold keep her from protesting. In the exhilarating atmosphere of the mountain retreat, the business world of San Diego and its restrictions seemed very far away.

They talked of trivial matters, though the words weren't at all important and they enjoyed the moments of silence just as fully. But the air was getting colder despite the heat from their bodies, and Kay shivered.

"Why didn't you tell me you were cold?" he asked, sitting straighter and removing his arm. "I'll spread the coals and pile the dishes in the kitchen. You go on back inside. A good shower will put some heat back into your bones."

Kay shivered again as he took his arm away, but she had to admit the shower sounded tempting. "What about you? I don't want you to get too cold," she said, drinking the last sip of her wine.

His arm came back up around her, his hand slowly tracing up the length of her arm, and a delightful tremor sped through her body. He pulled her closer and kissed the tender place in front of her ear. "Don't worry about me," he said, his voice a caress, "I'll manage." His tongue teased the outline of her ear before he added, "And don't hurry on my account."

She was out of her seat in a moment, the sensations he was causing leaving her breathless and irresolute. Why did she always falter at his merest touch? The tiniest remnant of her earlier decision had jolted her out of her seat, but now she found she was incapable of taking the first step away from his side.

"Go on, Kay," he said quietly, gently pushing her toward the kitchen door. The touch of his hand lingered on her body, propelling her with its radiant glow as she made her way through the lower portion of the house and up the steps to the loft.

The dirty jeans and her top were a formless mass against the light blue of the bathroom's rug as she stepped into the shower and reveled under its stinging rays. She gave herself a brisk scrubbing, and the remaining ugly patches of gray finally surrendered to the superior force of the loofah.

As she was lathering her hair with her eyes tightly closed, she felt a sudden draft of cold air. She groped blindly to feel if the door to the shower had somehow come open, but her hand didn't encounter the cool glass as she'd expected. Instead it fell upon warm, wet skin.

"Burke!" she said with a gasp, though she was disturbed to note she wasn't as surprised or as upset as she ought to be.

Hearing his sardonic chuckle, she tried to open her eyes to glare at him, but the shampoo ran into her eyes and she had to close them quickly and retreat under the sharp stinging water to rinse off her hair.

With her hair clinging to her head, she came back out from under the spray and put her hands on her hips. "Burke, just *what* do you think you're doing here?"

He grinned, and as he slowly let his eyes travel down her, she realized how difficult it was to give full vent to her anger when she didn't have any clothes on. She remained standing as she was, but the fire went out of her eyes.

"Taking a shower. I got as dirty as you did, so why waste water? This way we can both have a nice long hot shower."

"Well it may be nice, and it may be hot, but I can't guarantee how long it's going to be," Kay told him, leaning her head back to let the full force of the water play over her head.

Kay was lost in the shower's roar for only a moment before she felt a hand exploring the drenched skin of her waist. With her hair lying smoothly against her scalp and drops of water dripping off the ends of her lashes, she blinked at him in confusion while waiting for the strength to tell him to stop.

It never came and his hand continued its upward search until it reached the fullness of her breast. The soft, wet globe was held gently in his hand as his thumb traced the dark-pink flesh surrounding the growing nipple.

Was she to be forever at the mercy of his nearness, of his touch? She closed her eyes, feeling the now-familiar ball of fire starting its slow spin inside her. Why had no man ever made her feel this way? Made her feel . . . a gasp escaped her and she lost her train of thought as his thumb brushed lightly across the taut nipple.

Only Matt had ever gotten this close to her, and compared to Burke, he'd been a fumbling boy. But she knew instinctively that no others could have sparked to life the fire that spun within her. And as his hands followed the enticing contours of her body, that miniature sun spun faster and faster as if it were an ice skater who had drawn her arms close in to her body, surrendering to the momentum.

Facing him, the water pounding on her back, she reached out to brush water droplets from his shoulders, but her hand was held by the feel of iron velvet and she couldn't halt her hand's passage as it traveled down his chest to the hard muscles of his stomach. When her hand drifted even farther down, his voice came low and incoherent from deep inside his chest.

The planes of her hips seemed to fascinate him and his hands followed a trail from the small of her back around the fullness of her hips to the soft concave flesh of her stomach. Jets of flame were darting outward to lodge just below the surface of her skin, waiting to explode with a powerful urgency at his touch.

The drumming of the water added its counterbeat to the rhythm of the tiny explosions. He pulled her to him, his touch hotter than the water and his midnight eyes nearly closed with his passion as his impatient lips descended to hers.

Shuddering at the impact, she drew him nearer, her tongue licking up the tiny droplets from his lips. His wet mouth slid tantalizingly over hers and she pressed the full length of her wet body into his male frame. His tongue met and curled around hers, and she felt flares ignite deep inside of her; she was caught up in the maelstrom of their passion.

Rivulets of water flowed across her shoulders and his hungry mouth followed the twisting trail as if jealous of their freedom to roam her body. Then his lips found hers again and he kissed her with a passion and possession she willingly succumbed to. A delicious, spinning tension grew inside her, probing for the source of its release. Pressed to his hard masculine frame, her hips sensed the promise his body held and they pressed tighter into him.

"Let me love you, Kay," Burke said, the droplets on his

lashes forming a jeweled setting for the smoky sapphires of his eyes.

A laugh from deep within her throat wove around him and she twined her arms around his neck and whispered in his ear, her voice low with her own desire. "You are." She nibbled on the lobe of his ear and laughed again. "You are."

Reaching behind her, he turned off the spraying water. They stood for a moment with only their breathing and the water dripping from their bodies breaking the silence between them.

Her hand traced a tiny stream of water down the side of his face, but its course was interrupted as the door slipped open effortlessly and he quickly switched on the heat lamp to warm them. He wrapped an enormous bluegreen towel around her, drying her in his embrace. Only her face was uncovered and his hands held her head tenderly as his lips caressed her in a soft, yielding kiss. In that moment she knew she loved him.

The kiss deepened, their tongues exploring the burning interior of their mouths. Then his lips left her mouth and blazed an incandescent path along her neck and behind her ears. She leaned against him in response.

Her arms were around his shoulders and her hands felt the strong muscles contract as he picked her up and carried her into the bedroom, kissing her all the while. It was warm in the bedroom; he'd evidently turned on the heater before getting into the shower with her.

"Did you plan this?" she asked lightheartedly as he carried her toward the bed.

"I *hoped* for it," he answered, bending down to place her on the bed.

"Oh, Burke, no!" She laughed, hastily adding, when she felt him tense, "We'll ruin the comforter." Her hand caressed the skin at the base of his neck to reassure him.

Kneeling slowly, he carefully placed her on the thick lamb's wool rug on the floor next to the bed.

Seeing her smile as she sank into the depths of the fleece, he whispered, "All right?"

She nodded and drew him down to her, their lips meeting in a long, slow kiss that made her tremble. His hands stroked her sides with a long, smooth motion, his thumbs following the outline of her breasts.

Her own hands delighted in the movement of his muscles under her fingers and she lovingly caressed the two slight dimples at the small of his back. Her hands flowed down further to the small, hard mounds of his buttocks. She found the movement of the thick muscles there exciting as he put one of his legs over hers, and he groaned when she tightened her hold.

He was resting on one elbow now, and his tongue rapidly flicked her left nipple, the tall, taut knob sending spasms through her, making her back arch to urge her body closer to his. She knew he had long since been ready for her, and after gently brushing a few wet strands of hair from her face, he kissed her softly and deeply, covering her body with his and making them one.

She cried out at the shimmering heat that flared through her body, her hips moving gently of their own accord. Burke's breath caressed her face with a passionate counterrhythm that matched their movements.

Lost in a world of a building, pulsing fire, Kay didn't hear her low moans of pleasure as the flame reached ever higher toward the tiny ball of energy that spun faster and faster at the core of her. All of her attention was centered on that dizzying sun until fragments started spinning off, sending streamers of light and fire through her body.

A long, feminine cry filled the room as the tense star within her exploded in a nova of ecstasy, soon followed by a low masculine moan wrenched from the depths of Burke's throat.

Breathing in heavy gasps, Kay relaxed in the soft fleece and let the tingling remnants of pleasure lap against the confines of her body. Burke lay half on, half off her, and she could feel the rhythm of his breathing as he drank in the air.

She felt him kiss her again on the sensitive flesh in front of her ear. Turning, she looked at him, her spent desire turning her eyes to molten gold.

Smiling tenderly, he cooled her eyelids with a kiss. He kissed the bridge of her nose and then its tip, his mouth coming to rest on the deep rose lips, slightly swollen from her pleasure; his hand followed the flush from their lovemaking as it receded down her neck.

"Ah, my love, my sweet, sweet love," he whispered, his lips leaving a lambent path along her hairline. Kissing her deeply once again, he settled his body next to hers in a position comfortable for both of them.

Kay smiled at him, her hand reaching up to draw a finger over the tiny hairs that had dried and fallen in waves along his forehead.

The sensuous memory left her eyes nearly closed as she twirled a blond curl around her finger. The sensations that had washed over her could quickly become a habit, she knew. Drawing her hand down the contours of his arm, she felt the stirrings in a new niche deep inside of her where her craving for him had found a permanent home. After the deep, all-abiding pleasure he'd shown her, never would she be far from needing his touch.

But she shook her head to chase the thought of the future away; the present was all that mattered now.

They talked for a long while, occasionally taking a tiny nibble of one another as they discussed favorite symphonies or a particularly moving part in a well-liked play. A perfectly ordinary sentence would be interrupted by a quick kiss to the soft underside of his chin and then resumed. They lay there, wrapped in damp towels and each other's arms, with no thought of the time passing into the night.

After a deep, slow kiss, Burke raised himself up and looked down at her with a soft smile on his face. "When we get back, we'll go see a play at the new Old Globe, and have a quiet dinner. . . ." He stopped in midsentence as she placed a finger against his lips.

His talk of San Diego had sent a ripple of disquiet through her that she wasn't ready to acknowledge. "Shhh, don't talk of the future, only *now.*"

A few minutes later she shivered, but it was because of the encroaching chill of the room and not Burke's words. Rising to his knees, he gently wrapped the large towel back around her and helped her to her feet. Together they went back into the bathroom and finished drying their still-damp hair before crawling under the down comforter and falling asleep in a close embrace.

A distant ringing broke in on Kay's dreams. Shaking her head to make it go away and leave her to the pleasant visions didn't work, and she slowly returned to consciousness. She first became aware of the rumpled sheets beneath her and the pillow over her head, blocking out the sun. Just as she threw the latter toward the foot of the bed, the ringing stopped, and she was starting to relax in its absence when an indistinct voice intruded.

"Ticher, what the hell are you talking about! No one would give you the go-ahead. . . ."

Reality, and all it entailed, rushed in on Kay. All the dreams and soft pastel visions of her and Burke were shattered by the sunlight into a thousand glittering shards.

They could never make it together—one business person was difficult enough to deal with, but two! Impossible. And Burke's "occupation" of salvaging newly purchased companies for ESSCO would keep him on the move for a long time to come. Far away from Kay Pagel in San Diego. Perhaps he'd occasionally be in southern California and he'd stop by; but she couldn't—wouldn't!—live from visit to visit like some poor pathetic soul who wandered from handout to handout.

And he'd known their circumstances when he'd insisted

on bringing her to Big Bear, known she'd usually be safely tucked away in San Diego while he wandered the country. It wasn't jealousy of his traveling—she'd burned out whatever wanderlust had been in her soul in her first two years with Pagel Associates.

Instructional technologists went wherever the problem was—factory, airline terminals, or merchant ship—and she'd been to them all and more. It'd had been with a grateful sigh of relief that she'd hired Gloria and then Steve to do that rugged legwork.

Her fists were balled up under the comforter. Sure, Burke had known—but she'd known it, too, and still she'd let herself become involved with him. That she was working with him should have warned her away, but—oh, no!—a soft caress or two and she'd been a pushover for him. How *could* she have let herself get involved! She'd told herself to keep away, but had she listened?

Her glance raked the rug beside the bed and a flush stole up her cheeks as she recalled her passion from the night before. She hadn't listened with a vengeance.

Burke slammed down the receiver with a coarse oath. He stomped up the stairs, and she could see the anger glittering in his eyes before his foot fell on the first step; but she was ready to meet him.

"Damn it, Kay! You'd better go—"

"I'd better go what? Finish my report? What's the rush —do you want to drag me along on another of your escapades? Where are you planning on going this time?" she asked sarcastically. She was furious at him; she'd had quite enough of his commandeering ways and she told herself this was sign-off time.

Disgust at him, at herself, at their situation, overwhelmed her modesty and she threw back the sheet and walked quickly to the closet. His brows lowered in unpleasant surprise, but her glance was full of contempt as she searched for her robe.

"You are really good, Burke," she spat. "Just send in

Huntingdon anytime you need someone to take over, is that it? ESSCO really knew what they were doing when they hired you."

Her hands couldn't locate her robe, so she frantically went to the dresser and pulled out the first thing her hands landed on. It was an old French-cut T-shirt, its San Diego State logo cracking from age. It wasn't long enough to cover her nude body, but she dragged it over her head anyway.

Annoyed though she was at having to dress in front of him while he silently watched her, his hands on his hips, the firm thrust of her jaw didn't waver as she ransacked the drawer, grabbing a pair of lace panties and faded jeans that were fraying around the bottom. Jamming her legs into the jeans, she turned to face him.

"*Now* will you—" Burke began, his voice chilling her as if she'd dived into a pool of melted snow.

But she didn't give him a chance to finish. "I'll be back to finish your damned report later!" And with a pair of shoes in her left hand, she ran down the steps, grabbed her Windbreaker from the back of a chair, and slammed out the front door. She ignored his bellowed "*Kay!*" as the door crashed behind her.

The uneven asphalt of the mountain streets made walking difficult, but Kay wandered down short street after short street, not paying attention to her surroundings. It had rained again during the night and large standing puddles of water were everywhere. But she didn't notice the zigzagging pattern her feet automatically followed to stay dry.

The man was maddening, exasperating! He was quite content just to walk in and take over any and all lives that came in his path. Maybe it had become a habit with him, but if so, it was one habit she could do without. Clients should stay in their place—in an office, on the other side of a desk, preferably a large one!

She walked the physical roads with her feet as she mentally followed different avenues of action she could take. Most of her ideas were absurd and unrealistic and she discarded them as soon as they came to mind—and one was so completely fantastic, it even made her chuckle.

But she was going to have to do something. Wandering around the convoluted residential streets of Big Bear for several hours, she contemplated the complete project with Southey. It was probably going take several months from task analysis to end result—the improved performance of Southey's employees. She'd already noted in her report that a number of job aids were going to have to be designed as well as some restructuring done to the equipment itself.

And the last preliminary report she'd been working on had strongly indicated that formal classroom training was called for. She'd have to go through the entire report again, but if her instincts were right—and they usually were—that also meant multimedia support would probably be needed. And *that* meant video scripts would have to be written and produced and that overhead transparencies, slides, and flip-charts would all have to be designed and created.

Pagel Associates could handle all of it with ease. But Burke was going to have to be made to understand that anything *other* than professional training and support was out of the question.

Kay loved her work and thinking of it made her adrenaline flow again. She was ready to get back to her report.

Nothing more romantic than a demanding stomach roused her out of her reverie and, to her dismay, she was completely lost. The landmarks were all unfamiliar: a house made of rough-hewn logs sat next to a tall, narrow A-frame which sat next to a snug little cottage of knotty pine trimmed with gingerbread flourishes that had been painted white.

She stood very still and tried to hear the sound of the traffic on the main road to get her bearings, but the trees and houses absorbed sounds. Even noise from as close as a street away could only faintly be heard.

One resident had placed large, tree-length logs around his yard and Kay reluctantly sat down and tried to reconstruct her meanderings. Hoping that any street going down would eventually lead her to the town, she decided to keep walking.

Rising to carry out her decision, she took a step and stopped. The sight of a car pulling into the narrow lane caught her eye and she sighed with a mixture of frustration and relief as she recognized the elegant red lines of Burke's Porsche. Kay sat back down on the log to wait for him.

The low-slung sports car pulled up in front of her. She watched him through the dark tinted windows as he leaned over the passenger seat and opened the door for her. The softness of the car's seat felt wonderful after the hard bark of the log and she reveled in it until Burke's harsh voice interrupted her thoughts.

"You'd better call Gloria Larson," he said, his face cold and forbidding.

The set of his face made her wary. Why did she need to call Gloria? "What's wrong, Burke? Did Gloria call?"

His expression was harsher than she'd ever seen it. Making a series of short turns to return them home, he parked the car in the muddy driveway before answering.

"No."

"Burke, what the hell is going on? You sit there like some great tribal god answering in monosyllables and not telling me anything. Has something happened at Southey? If this project's been postponed again, I'll take Southey to court!" Kay warned him, her voice low as she spat out the words.

"Don't start threatening me with what Pagel Associates is going to do until you find out how much of Pagel Associates there is left!" he said, slamming the door and walking up to the house without waiting for her.

129

She scrambled out of the car and ran into the house after him, the pit of her stomach tightening in fear. What could he possibly mean?

Kay entered the house as he was going up the steps to the loft, the strong muscular back, which her fingers so vividly recalled, facing her. He couldn't see the anxiety that riddled her body.

She only hesitated a moment. Hurrying to the phone, she punched Pagel's number ferociously and turned to watch him disappear around the corner of the loft. Anger warred with trepidation inside of her: anger at his abrupt dismissal of her question and fear as to why she needed to call Gloria.

Her secretary answered on the third ring.

"Kay! Thank God you've called! Hang on a minute," Mary Duncan told her in a rush. Mary incompletely put her hand over the phone's mouthpiece, and Kay could hear her shout, "*Gloria, it's Kay!*" A whispered "darn!" was quickly followed by another shout: "Jackie! Go catch Gloria and tell her Kay's on the phone!"

A breathless Mary came back on the line and said, "Gloria will be here in just a second. We've been trying to get you all morning!"

"What on earth is going on?" Kay finally was able to ask.

"It's really complicated. Wait, here's Gloria," Mary told her. The receiver changed hands and Gloria's low, no-nonsense voice came on the line.

"Kay, thank goodness you called! Your phone's been busy every time I tried to get you, until I finally got through and nobody answered!"

"Gloria! What's happening?" Kay demanded, anger and fear making her stomach tighten painfully.

"Some guy named Ticher from Southey has been trying to bribe your people away. He's really starting to hassle some of them—phone calls at night and all. And he even offered Steve twice what he's getting here. Steve turned him down, but some of them can't afford to turn down offers like that. This is getting beyond what I can handle."

Kay felt her blood freeze in her veins. Ticher! Wasn't he the one Burke had been talking to just that morning? "Has anyone actually left? What have you done to put a stop to it? Have you called Southey?" Kay said, firing her questions rapidly as she took command.

"So far only Patterson's left—no great loss—but the money's sounding awfully good to some of them. I put in some heated calls to Huntingdon this morning when I couldn't raise you, but he won't answer," Gloria told her. "That nasty secretary of his says he's not in, but won't say where he *is!* I gave her some pretty warm words herself, but no go. Can't locate him to get him to call off his hound."

"I'll take care of Bur—Huntingdon. You work on Ticher. Threaten to call the police and get a court injunction against his coming near Pagel. And if that doesn't work, make good the threat and call 'em. I'll be there in three hours, flat."

After making a few more arrangements with Gloria, Kay slammed the receiver down in its cradle and dragged out the phone book. Throwing the Yellow Pages open to "Automobiles, Rental and Leasing," she picked the receiver back up and had started to punch the first number on the list when it was wrenched out of her grasp.

"What do you think you're doing?" he asked, hanging the phone up none too gently. He was still dressed as he had been when he'd walked in—he hadn't even bothered to take off his flannel jacket.

"What does it look like? I'm renting a car and going back to San Diego. That shouldn't surprise you too much." Her topaz eyes were glittering with a cold, hard gaze as she reached for the phone.

He grabbed her wrist, pulling her to him until her body was resting against his. But she fiercely schooled her reactions and didn't let her flesh yield to his touch. She was cold inside, an arctic wind blowing through her heart as she thought of what she had almost allowed this man to do to her company.

"Let me go," she said to him, her seething anger giving a steel edge to her voice. But she refused to struggle.

"You don't need to rent a car when there's a perfectly good one out in the driveway. I'll drive you back."

"Let me go."

"Kay, there's no reason not to go with me. What do you think I'm going to do? Abandon you in Sun City?"

"Let me go."

"Damn it!" he swore, releasing her with a shove that sent her falling back onto the sofa. "You've got fifteen minutes to pack."

She glanced at the phone once more, then discarded the idea of renting a car. Even if he was working against her, she didn't think he'd do anything drastic and she'd get to San Diego a lot quicker if she rode down with him. Striding purposefully to the loft, she neatly sidestepped his suitcase on the top step.

Dragging her own two pieces of luggage out of the closet, she had completely, if not neatly, finished her packing in ten minutes. Hauling them down to the side door, she stopped off in the kitchen, then went to the dining-room table and swept the stacks of notes and reports into one big pile. Stuffing the mounds of paper into a grocery sack, she carefully folded it closed and tucked it under her arm. This was one project Southey wasn't going to forget!

Burke came in from inspecting the car and walked to the loft steps to get his bag—staring at her with his arm extended. Kay relinquished the sack with her report, but watched him closely as he deposited it behind the passenger seat.

Coming back in, he said, "If you're not planning on visiting again soon, I suggest you close the place up tightly."

Nodding, she headed for the kitchen, her mouth set in

a firm line. When Burke followed her in a few minutes, she was pouring the rest of the milk down the drain, running cold water to rise out the sink as she did so.

"When you're done there, let me know, and I'll turn off the water and check the circuit breakers," Burke said.

"Fine," was all she answered, reaching to turn on the garbage disposal and assist their leftovers down the growling drain.

"Kitchen's done." She had gone back out into the living room, where he was closing the blinds with a quick jerk after making sure the windows were locked.

"Fine," he mimicked, and went on closing the blinds. A few minutes after he'd gone back into the kitchen, the lights in the loft went out and the ticking of the electric clock on the living room wall stopped.

It was eerie standing in the shuttered, darkened cabin. She noticed a bright patch of light flickering at her feet, and faced the open side door to see the sun trying desperately to break through. But the gray clouds jealously bullied the enfeebled sun to retreat and the dim, muted sky reflected her own depression. The heat her body had generated during the brisk walk had dissipated, leaving a cold, frozen lump in her chest.

Burke walked back into the room and watched her silently for a moment. Quietly, he said, "I put the grill in the storage shed and locked the back door. Everything's locked up tight, except the side door."

Kay found her anger had flown. It was useless to be angry at him—he was a businessman doing what he got paid to do. The thought left a melancholy note, which she couldn't brush aside. She wasn't angry anymore; in fact she felt nothing at all.

His blue eyes were dark and unreadable in the dim light; her own gold eyes were veiled, as if protecting her thoughts from intruders. He reached up to brush away a wisp of hair, but she turned her head from his touch and stepped back. His arm dropped.

Lifting up a slat of the blinds to look out, Kay saw the drizzle had begun again. How appropriate that the world should cry when her heart wanted to weep along with it. Kay hadn't had a good soul-wrenching cry in years, but she suddenly discovered the need to curl up in a corner and cry for hours.

"Has it started to rain yet?" Burke's voice broke through her reverie and she shook herself.

Why did she feel so empty inside? "It just started drizzling," she told him. She saw him narrow his eyes at her toneless reply, but ignored him.

The small phone-book was still on the coffee table and he flipped to the front of it. A few seconds later he punched in a number and stood with the handset held to his ear. Kay turned back to look out the window.

Burke came and stood close to her, his hands stuffed in his pockets and a look of frustration on his face. "Highway 138's closed; a mud slide just passed the Crestline turnoff. We'll have to sidetrack through the desert."

"Then, let's go," she said, walking away from him without a glance. "I want to get to San Diego by four."

The gravel spun under the Porsche's wheels as Burke gunned the car out of the driveway. He hadn't said a word to her since he'd followed her out of the house, slamming the door behind him. His hands kept gripping the wheel, loosening and clenching in a pattern that matched the tightening of the muscle in his jaw.

"Kay," he said, "what Ticher did was out of bounds as far as Southey—and ESSCO—are concerned. ESSCO's dealings may not always be angelic, but they're always aboveboard."

Giving vent to a snort of derision, Kay twisted in her seat away from him. "Not always angelic? Not always ethical, you mean! Look, Burke, when I started Pagel Associates, I wasn't some bright-eyed idiot with dreams of glory where the good guys always wear white hats. I wasn't a fool then, and I'm not a fool now."

She grimaced at the memory of her recent actions and amended herself. "Not much of a fool, anyway. I tried to run my own company with ethical, moral considerations that ESSCO seems to blithely ignore. ESSCO and their best trained hounds *always* keep their eyes on the almighty bottom line!"

"Enough! Dammit, I told you what Ticher did was *not* approved by ESSCO! He's from the old group George Southey had gathered around him before deciding to sell out to us." Burke's grip on the wheel was murderous and Kay experienced a momentary flutter in her stomach when she thought it was really her neck he'd like to have that death-grip on.

"It must be very convenient to have all those old employees to blame when a job gets bungled."

The landmarks they were passing on their way out of the mountain town were unfamiliar and Kay was unexpectedly relieved. The drive into Big Bear at midnight had taken on a rosy, dreamlike quality, and even though the dream had turned into a nightmare, its beginning was still special to her.

Burke didn't answer her and the silence between them grew palpable as the car wound around Baldwin Lake on its way down the mountain. He was taking the corners too fast and Kay decided not to say anything to break his concentration—at least she hoped those deep grooves in his forehead meant he was concentrating on the road.

They left the lake behind and peaked over the edge of Bear Valley. Now they were actually heading down the "Grapevine" toward the desert town of Lucerne Valley that lay scattered at the base of the range. Kay'd heard about the infamous road, but she'd never had the urge to try it. Now she had no choice.

The short stretch of straightaway suddenly ended with a sharp turn to the right and Kay braced herself to keep from being thrown against Burke. The tires whined their protest.

135

The road wound back to the left and Kay was thrown hard against the door. She tried closing her eyes and clutching the shoulder strap of her seat belt—the only secure thing in a world grown terrifying—but her stomach cried out its complaint.

Her eyes opened to see a camper careening into the Porsche's path. A stifled scream escaped her before Burke swerved to the dirt shoulder at the same time the camper was yanked back into its own lane.

"Aren't you going to stop?" she cried. But Burke only slowed the car down on the shoulder; she felt the slight bump as he pulled back onto the asphalt. Accelerating back up to speed, Burke took the downhill hairpin turns with a devilish glint in his eyes.

He must be possessed! She held on to her seat tightly to keep from being thrown back and forth like a tennis ball as Burke pushed the Porsche to its limits, taking the corners with little slackening of speed and whipping it around the next turn. It was a very long half-hour.

CHAPTER EIGHT

At last they passed the Pfizer plant that marked the end of the twisting road and entered the gentle downward slope that led to Lucerne Valley and the Mojave Desert. When they reached the small town, Burke pulled into a corner gas station that was a refugee from an earlier time. Coats of paint on the small stuccoed building had flaked off to reveal geologic strata of faded colors.

"I've got to make a phone call," he told her, throwing the car keys to the station attendant before walking to the lone phone booth at the edge of the station's property.

Reaction set in and Kay was shaking down to her bones. She had to get out! Her hand was on the door handle when awareness of her surroundings broke down her wall of panic and she saw four rough, scraggly cowboys standing near an ancient pickup, watching her with predatory eyes. She sat back in her seat, her hand falling useless to her lap.

A stab of despair lunged through her, making her feel all too acutely the loss of the moments of happiness she'd spent with Burke. But she now knew he wasn't really the kind of man she'd thought she'd known the past week. That man was an illusion created expressly for her benefit, an illusion she'd fallen in love with . . . *no!* A momentary passion was *not* love!

Her eyes wandered to Burke, standing in front of the open booth. One hand was on his hip, his feet slightly apart in a stance that effectively proclaimed his confidence and power. How could she have thought she felt that deeply for him? She wasn't an adolescent to fall in love with every tall, blond, blue-eyed, well-formed man whose muscles rippling under her fingers sent flames licking downward through her body. Stop it! What was she thinking?

Burke violently hung up the phone and stalked back toward the car. The cowboys stood to snickering at him until Burke stopped and glared back with such malevolence that Kay thought he was going to jump into their midst, with fists flying, at any moment. They evidently thought so as well, because they looked at the ground, then turned the other way.

"I don't know if I did any good, but I tried," he told her as he paid the attendant and gunned the car to life, his impatience making the car screech out onto the road.

"I think those cretins got the message," she said. He looked at her oddly for a moment and glanced in his rearview mirror. Glancing back at her, he tightened his mouth into a thin line and returned his eyes to the road.

At three forty-five they entered San Diego's city limits and Kay sighed with relief. The trip back had not been anything like the one up to the mountain town; their conversation had been desultory and after a few sentences would quickly grind to a halt for lack of momentum.

"Do you remember how to get to my place?" she asked.

"I was going to swing by and drop you off at your office," he said. His eyes were on the road and he didn't see the look of disgust she sent him.

"Wonderful. Let all my employees know that while they've been valiantly fighting off an attack from Southey's *second* in command, the president of Pagel Associates has been spending a rapturous week in the arms of Southey's *first* in command!"

He gave her a sidelong look that could have meant anything. Nodding, he said, "Okay, I'll drop you off at your condo. It'll give you a chance to change, too."

"Thank you."

A half an hour later a taxi deposited her in front of the double glass doors that led into the suite of offices occupied by Pagel Associates. As she pushed open one of the doors, a blast of air-conditioned air hit her at the same time a cheer went up from a group of her employees clustered around Mary Duncan's desk.

"Kay! Thank goodness you're back!" Gloria came around from behind the desk and put an arm around her, giving her a squeeze. "Have we missed you! I sure haven't got your savvy when it comes to dealing with these people."

Steve, his dark-brown hair as shaggy as ever, grinned his welcome and put out his hand. "Glad you're back. It's been fun, but—whew!—I wouldn't want to do it every day! Just last night I turned down the cost of the elusive Huntingdon's fancy sports car! Boy, did that ever hurt!"

In the general welcoming cheer Kay didn't think anyone noticed how forced her smile became when Steve mentioned Burke. She looked around at the laughing faces and felt heartsick.

They'd been sticking by her, giving up dreams of maybe getting enough together to make a down payment on a house or—glancing at Cathy's body swollen by eight months of pregnancy—that much-needed new station wagon; and how had she repaid their loyalty? She'd been *sleeping* with the president of the very company they were fighting against!

"It's good to be back," she told them. She could feel rationality flooding back into her brain as she took over her rightful place. "Why don't you take off early today? I need to talk with Gloria, find out how things stand, and then decide what we can do."

She started walking toward her office, but some inner urge nudged her and she stopped and turned back to face them. "It may be that it's just Ticher doing this on his own. He's one of George Southey's old team; he's not from ESSCO."

Obviously thinking the explanation left a lot to be desired, they nodded politely and, slightly embarrassed, Kay walked purposefully into her office.

"What made you say a thing like that?" Gloria asked after the door had closed behind her.

Kay sat heavily in her chair, considering what she should tell Gloria. She remained silent for several seconds, her fingers steepling, but then remembered she'd seen Burke do the same thing and hastily clenched her hands in her lap. She knew Gloria was primarily responsible for keeping her staff from bolting at the first scent of higher pay, and because of that—and her friendship—she deserved to know everything. Kay blanched at the thought.

"Gloria, I said it because that was the explanation Burke Huntingdon gave me."

"Huntingdon! I knew you could flush him out. Where'd you find him?" Gloria asked, smiling a smile that showed her respect for Kay Pagel's abilities.

"I, I . . ." She couldn't tell her! But she had to; she owed it to Gloria. Her old friend deserved to know what kind of woman she was working for.

Starting again, she said, "Gloria, I spent the week—" The phone interrupted her and she grabbed it guiltily, knowing her relief showed in her face.

"This is Burke," the deep voice on the other end of the line said. "How soon can you make it over here?"

"Twenty minutes," Kay answered. She put her hand over the mouthpiece and whispered to Gloria, "It's Huntingdon." The older woman's eyebrows shot up in surprise; then, as she watched the changes in Kay's face they lowered and her eyes narrowed.

"Bring a couple of your people, maybe Larson and Sterling. Scarp came down from L.A. and we'd like to ask Ticher some questions while you're here."

"Okay, we'll be there shortly," Kay promised. Looking at Gloria after she'd hung up the phone, she discovered her friend watching her closely. Kay opened her mouth to ask if something was wrong but changed her mind and said, "Get Steve. We're to meet Huntingdon at Southey in twenty minutes. He's got someone down from ESSCO headquarters in L.A."

Kay reached for the phone again, this time to call her lawyer. Quickly explaining the situation to her, Kay got the go-ahead on the visit, but was admonished to watch what she agreed to.

"Let's go," Kay said, hanging up again.

Gloria nodded and rose from her seat. Kay was following behind her when the younger woman faltered and stopped. "Ah, Gloria, could we take your car? Mine broke down." She couldn't meet Gloria's eyes and concentrated on the signed Ansel Adams print on the wall instead.

"No problem, Kay," Gloria said, her head cocked to one side in curiosity. "But we'd better hurry if we're going to catch Steve—you sent everyone home early, remember?"

The young man was still hunched over his desk finishing up a final exercise for one of the training courses he was developing. His dark eyes lit up at the chance to go to Southey and he was out of his chair and halfway down the hall before they caught up with with him.

It was shortly after five when the trio from Pagel Associates walked through the large wooden doors of the corporate office building, heading straight for the bank of elevators.

Steve gleefully punched "15" at Kay's request and they were soon marching down the thickly carpeted hallway to the ceiling-high burl door at the end. Nodding briefly at the stony-faced secretary, Kay walked on past and knocked rapidly at the door. A terse voice bade them enter.

Her contingent obeyed, but Kay felt her courage falter when she saw Burke standing by the dark windows towering over a short man with brown-gray hair. An older man with a liberal streaking of gray in what remained of his dark hair stood alone off to one side.

Burke looked up from his conversation and gave her a long, considering look. She returned his look with a frosty one of her own, and the silence stretched out until it threatened to become noticeable.

"Dr. Pagel." He nodded.

She returned his nod. "Mr. Huntingdon."

Without waiting for an introduction the short man next to Burke walked toward her, his hand extended in greeting. "So you're Dr. Pagel. I'm very pleased to meet you at last, though I'm sorry it had to be over such an unfortunate matter." He glanced quickly to the man in the corner, a frown lowering his mouse-brown, bushy eyebrows, then looked back at Kay.

Burke quietly joined them. "Robert," he said, speaking to the man standing next to Kay, "why don't we adjourn to the conference room next door, and then I can introduce you to *everyone* and we can get started."

Kay flushed at the veiled criticism of her monopolizing the ESSCO man's time. And it hadn't even been her fault! She was careful not to get too close to Burke as he politely herded them into the next room, the sulking man in the corner trailing behind them.

After they'd seated themselves in the chocolate-brown leather chairs around the large oak conference table, the introductions were completed. The short man was who Kay had thought: Robert Scarp, an unspecified executive with the ESSCO corporation. But the way the balding man kept casting Scarp wary glances and the way Burke deferred to him, Kay guessed Scarp was high up in the corporate hierarchy.

Scarp took command after a short private conversation with Burke. The latter sat back in his chair, as if he planned to be only an observer and not a participant, and Kay found his eyes resting on her more often than she'd have liked during the meeting.

"Well, let's get this unpleasantness over with," Scarp began, his mobile brows crawling up his forehead. "Dr. Pagel, ESSCO Corporation would like to apologize formally for this unwarranted attack on your company."

Kay bowed her head slowly in acceptance; if they were going to play the game this way—so would she.

They began an in-depth discussion of how Ticher had actually tried to woo Pagel's employees away. It seemed inducements of money, promotions, and even threats to professional reputations weren't beyond him, and Kay was appalled at what her employees had been made to suffer.

Kay's brow was furrowed in a frown. "But, Mr. Ticher, I still don't see what you had to gain by all of this . . . maneuvering. What could it gain you or Southey Manufacturing?"

"Ol' George never would've let outsiders come snooping around the place," Ticher said in his wheezing voice. "What Southey Manufacturing did was nobody's business but ours! You couldn't do the job you were contracted to do without your people, you know. And if they were hired by Southey there wasn't any problem. Perfect. And after you two left town, it was easy." His rude laugh ended with a coughing spasm.

Clearing his throat in the silence that greeted Ticher's statement, Scarp's eyebrows seesawed back and forth as he looked from Burke to Kay and then back to Burke.

"Yes, well, I believe Dr. Pagel was in Big Bear working on the preliminary analysis," he said. "And Mr. Huntingdon was out of town on a trip for ESSCO."

A trip for ESSCO! She'd been set up! Burke had said he'd told everyone he was on vacation! He had set her up like some plump pigeon just waiting to be picked off. Kay's eyes frosted over, sending an icy dagger toward Burke. But the ice in her eyes was nothing compared to the coldness that had rumbled through her heart like an avalanche.

She felt hollow inside. Through all her suspicions, a tiny, stubborn ray of hope had remained that somehow it had all been a misunderstanding. The ray winked out and left only a cold, dark emptiness behind.

Scarp went on, addressing Kay personally, though he seemed a bit taken aback at the cold, implacable gaze that met his genial gray-brown eyes. "We, both ESSCO and Southey Manufacturing, would like Pagel Associates to continue with this project while our lawyers work out an acceptable agreement between our companies. I know it's an awkward arrangement at best, but Mr. Huntingdon"—here Scarp nodded toward him, the expressive brows climbing even higher—"has assured me that your work is of exceptionally high quality and worth retaining. He particularly commended the work of you, Ms. Larson, and you, Mr. Sterling."

Gloria's eyebrows vied with Scarp's at that comment, trying to see how high a set of brows could travel up a person's forehead, as she looked at Kay with an incredulous expression on her face. But Kay's face remained a set mask and Gloria soon controlled her features.

"Mr. Ticher," Scarp continued, his brows crashing down almost to cover his eyes as he looked at the man slumping in his chair, "Mr. Ticher will be dealt with." Scarp turned back to Kay, his brows assuming a sort of middle ground. "Now, will that be to your satisfaction, Dr. Pagel? This training project is very important to Southey and, of course, to ESSCO. Improved production is an excellent way to improve profits, and *that*, Dr. Pagel, is the bottom line."

Kay unconsciously shifted her metallic gaze from Scarp's ragged features to Burke's. Their eyes locked, and although his face told her nothing, his head dipped almost imperceptibly to acknowledge the hit.

Steve rustled in his chair, causing Kay to glance toward him. Both he and Gloria were watching her, Gloria with a curious look. Kay lowered her eyes to her black matte pen trimmed in gold, which she had absently picked up during Scarp's speech.

She felt as if she were some third party watching the scene around the conference table play itself out from a distance. But her rational mind, like a distant puppet master, moved the strings. Her façade was undisturbed and the play went on as she heard herself answer.

"Mr. Scarp, naturally everything I say will have to be approved by our lawyer, but if she agrees to your arrangement, I have no objections. The project is a challenging one and I think *all* of us would be sorry to see it summarily stopped. I think Ms. Larson and Mr. Sterling will both agree with me—it's very difficult to be taken off a project before it's completed."

"Excellent, Dr. Pagel, and thank you," Scarp said. His brows were bobbing back and forth as a smile split his face.

Standing, he said, "It's been very nice meeting you all, but now I believe Mr. Ticher and I should be going. Burke can help you get started again." And then, shaking their hands, Scarp left with Ticher in tow.

Several minutes passed before a word was spoken by those left in the room. Steve looked uncomfortable, as if knowing something was wrong, but not really wanting to find out what. Gloria had the look of someone desperately trying to puzzle out a mystery without all the facts; Kay didn't enlighten her.

Burke's eyes narrowed as he looked at Kay. She could see, even seated several seats away from him, that his eyes were an opaque blue, no longer the transparent color of a mountain lake, but more the that of the murky, churning depths of a tumultuous river roaring down a steep, rocky path.

A day earlier she could easily have become lost in that whirling current, but now she shook off his influence and returned his look without a qualm beneath the cool amber surface of her eyes.

Clearing his throat, Burke launched into his plans for continuing Pagel's project. Steve and Gloria were soon adding their own comments, though Kay said little. But it was a profitable hour, and they came to terms at last on how the project would now be handled.

Near the end of the meeting the men's ties had been loosened and jackets hung over the backs of chairs. They were casually clustered around one end of the conference table, Burke sitting down, drawing out a sketch for the others as Kay leaned forward in her chair diagonally across from him.

Steve was standing to one side of the blond man, pointing out an objection. "That's pretty close to what I had in mind, Mr. Huntingdon, but I was thinking more—" He broke off, trying to locate a pen. Burke offered him his own slim gold pen, but Steve waved it away. "That's okay, thanks. The design stage is still a ways off, so it doesn't matter right now anyway." His dark eyes looked longingly at the drawing and Kay could see he was itching to get started on the real training work.

"A ways off?" Burke asked. "Why?"

"Why?" Gloria repeated before Steve could answer. "Because we've got a pesky task analysis to get out of the way and a report to write on it first! That's why."

"But I expect that report on my desk Monday afternoon," Burke said.

"What!" Gloria cried. "That's impossible!"

"No way," Steve added. "That's not nearly enough time!"

"Damn it, Burke," Kay said over the voices of the others, her anger overriding her control over her tongue, "you know it can't possibly be ready then. Give me until Tuesday at least!"

"Kay, you told me it was almost finished!" Burke answered. "We've got to get on with this project."

"Burke . . ." Kay began, then stopped. Her two employees were silently watching her with surprised looks on their faces. Kay's heart sank further as she saw Gloria's eyes wandered to Burke, no doubt noting the slight flush on his face, and then back to her employer, her eyes widening in shock. Steve was fiddling with his tie, trying to readjust it without a mirror, and he let his eyes travel past her unfocused.

"Gloria," Burke said, breaking into the silence, "I understood that Kay had been working on this report during her time in . . . away."

"I believe so," she answered hesitantly, looking at Kay for confirmation.

Kay thought her neck would break but she nodded affirmatively while her mind refused to consider all the harm she had almost caused.

"Good. But I *can* give you until Tuesday to get it finished. Then, Steve, you can start on the design phase. I'm very interested in seeing some more of your ideas."

Gloria and Steve relaxed and the tendrils of fear that had wrapped around Kay's spine began to recede. She knew Burke had deliberately used their first names to cover up the gaffe, but why should she thank him? He'd caused the problem in the first place; let him handle it.

The meeting ended a short while later and Kay offered to treat Steve and Gloria to dinner at one of the superb restaurants on Harbor Island. They settled on the Green Parrot, a delightful restaurant specializing in seafood with a Latino flavor.

At the end of the meal Kay plunked down her American Express card with all the evidence of good cheer, part of which was caused by the two enormous Margaritas she'd consumed. But she knew the rest was the role she'd chosen to play and she was wary of her own ability to carry it off; her control was stretched almost to the breaking point. Her wariness continued until the taillights of Gloria's car disappeared around the corner from her condo. She sighed and began to relax.

Fumbling in her purse, she'd pulled out her keys with

a victorious "Ah-hah!" when a car door closed nearby and footsteps brought someone nearer.

"Let me do that for you," Burke's voice said as he mounted the steps and stood close behind her. Gently taking the keys from her motionless hand, he quickly opened the door. A warm hand on the small of her back propelled her forward into the living room.

She continued to a chair and unceremoniously dumped her purse and briefcase into it. She balled her fist in front of her, squeezing so tightly her knuckles turned white. Gloria could have seen him! Did he mean to make sure her employees knew the depth of her perfidy? She wouldn't let him do that; her company was worth more than ten Burke Huntingdons! She wouldn't even let herself think about him.

When it became clear she was not going to turn around, he came up behind her. His hands gripped her shoulders and she felt his lips kiss her neck through her hair.

Stepping out of his grasp, she went to her stereo and began rapidly going through her collection of albums; she hadn't looked at him since he'd arrived. She should face him and tell him his little charade was over, tell him to leave. But she didn't turn around and she said nothing. Her trembling hands made it difficult to grasp the records.

The only sound in the room was of records being violently thrown on a reject stack. *Plop* went Tchaikovsky's Piano Concerto No. 1, *plop* went Gershwin's *Rhapsody in Blue*, *plop plop plop* went three albums in her precious early Beatles collection.

"Kay!" Burke's voice came from behind her. "I came by to let you know what ESSCO's going to do about Ticher."

Plop went another early album.

"*Kay!* Will you listen to me?"

She lifted up the dust cover to her turntable and saw him approaching. Frowning, she frantically pulled out the record from the jacket she was holding and quickly put it on, letting the needle fall where it would. Just as he grabbed her shoulders and turned her around to face him, the pulsing primal beat of a song by the Doors filled the room.

Burke towered over her, his hands alternately gripping and releasing her shoulders in his agitation, his face bent close to hers.

She saw that face, his jaw set and his eyes burning with a cobalt fire, she smelled the tantalizing mixture of scents that proclaimed him to be Burke Huntingdon and no other. And when Jim Morrison's deep, sensual voice started assaulting her ears with all the urgency of a decade earlier, her senses were almost overrun.

Burke's grip on her shoulders tightened as his mouth descended to hers, but she wrenched away, turning around in panic and scraping the needle across the record with a loud rip in her haste to keep it from playing. Her senses couldn't take the continuing assault.

"Woman," Burke forced out between gulps of air. "Woman, what is wrong with you?" He grabbed her around the waist to pull her to him, but she twisted away from him, her blouse coming out of her waistband as she did so.

"Leave me alone," she said in a tone of cold fury.

"The great pristine citadel is once more intact, is that it?" His disgust at her blazed out of his eyes. "Recess is over and now it's back to work! If that's the way you want it, Dr. Pagel, that's the way you've got it."

The windows rattled in their frames as he slammed the door. She heard the Porsche gunned to life and the squeal of the tires as he sped out of the drive. Trembling with reaction, she felt something inside of her crack and she sank to the floor where she was, great heaving sobs racking her body as her heart and soul cried out their anguish.

Several hours later she awoke to find the room lit with an eerie green glow. Her eyes were puffy and swollen and her lips bruised and feeling twice their normal size. Groggily she drew herself to her knees and reached out to turn off the stereo receiver.

Instantly she was in darkness. Remembering the automatic light switch she'd hooked up to the living-room lamp, she unplugged it with shaking hands to keep it from coming on.

Sore and exhausted at this sudden opening of her emotional floodgates, she leaned her head wearily down on her arm on the end table and gathered the strength to stand. Eventually she managed to drag herself into the bedroom, swaying on her feet as she pulled her blouse the rest of the way out of her waistband, finishing the job Burke had started. Dumping that, her pants, and her underclothes on a nearby chair, she threw herself across the bed.

Minutes passed as she lay there in the darkness, careful to keep her mind a blank, before expending that last bit of energy and crawling between the sheets.

She didn't wake up until eleven the following day. Appalled at the unusually late hour even for a Saturday, she forced herself to get out of bed, even though her body and mind were still groggy from their emotional wrenching. She stumbled into the bathroom, cranking on the shower and standing under its stinging cold rays until some semblance of consciousness emerged.

Leaning over as she vigorously rubbed her wet hair with a towel, she could feel the blood rushing to her head. She rubbed harder, hoping to make some of those brain cells she hadn't heard from lately start to work again. Her emotions were in a curiously suspended state, and though the coldness had gone, it had been replaced by nothing.

But she doubted her feelings would stay hidden for long; one day soon they were going to break out with a vengeance unless she got herself back in control.

Perhaps she should let herself go out with some men whom she found challenging, instead of the eager-to-please but boring Ric Adlers of the world. The thought that Burke Huntingdon was all the challenge she'd ever need was quickly pushed away.

When she had finished drying her hair, she strode across her bedroom and threw open the closet doors. Glancing out the window, she saw it was overcast and picked out a pair of polished cotton brown pants that had a look of leather to them and topped it with a cream-colored tuxedo-pleated shirt with wide dolman sleeves that tapered to narrow cuffs. The outfit gave her a swashbuckling air and she grinned at the lift she felt as she stuffed the narrow legs of the pants into black knee-high leather boots with three-inch heels.

Standing in front of her dresser mirror with her legs apart and her hands on her hips, she looked straight into her golden eyes and gave the image a steady stare.

"You are *not* going to give up everything you've worked for for a man who uses any tactic in the book to achieve his ends," she told herself firmly. There was no response.

She tried again. "Let's be honest, shall we? Yes, he takes you—correction—he takes your *body* where it's never been before, but is *that* worth destroying your reputation over?" She waited for the woman in the mirror to answer as her mind ran over the times he had taken her to those wonderful places of colliding stars and exploding atoms. Blinking her eyes and giving her head a tiny shake, she belatedly forced out an answer. "Of course not!"

Looking closely, Kay admitted that the bright, in-command young woman staring out at her had puffy, pink-rimmed eyes and looked as though she'd spent the night on a crying jag. Which she had. Kicking a stray sandal out of the way, she slumped out of her stance and sat down on the edge of the bed.

She'd been angry and upset last night, but now she felt as if she'd been stuffed with cotton like a new bottle of aspirin. All of her emotions were in stasis and she felt numb.

Getting up to fix breakfast, she kept telling herself over

and over all the reasons why she should hate, dislike, and loathe the man, trying to work up a healthy contempt for him. But there wasn't even a ripple of a response.

The litany of his wrongs continued, but dialing her sister-in-law to tell her she'd returned from Big Bear, Kay was disappointed to find it wasn't working well at all.

Her brother answered and their conversation made a temporary foray into her benumbed state, but after she'd hung up and then called Mary Duncan to see if she could go into the office to work, the feeling of no feeling returned.

Mary agreed to the overtime, so Kay gathered up her briefcase, and taking a couple of cans of diet soda and an apple from the refrigerator, headed for her office to work on the report. The litany against Burke was forgotten.

The door to her office was left open to help them keep each other company in the otherwise deserted building and the soft whisper of air through the vents was punctuated by the faint rasping of the word processor's keyboard as Mary's fingers flew over the keys.

Working on the report held Kay's interest for several minutes until her thoughts drifted to the scene the night before with Burke. Unconsciously chewing on the end of her pencil, she sat back in disgust and threw the pencil down on the yellow pad in front of her.

What was wrong with her? It wasn't the first time she'd imagined herself in love with someone. It didn't happen often, naturally, but still, it shouldn't have sent all her emotions into hiding.

Picking up the pencil again, she determinedly started writing, refusing to think of her own reactions. Now wasn't the time to consider them; wait until the gnawing emptiness had subsided. But she worked out of habit, with little motivation other than that it was something she'd set up for herself to do.

Calling it quits late Saturday, Mary agreed to come back in on Sunday. On the following day Kay worked methodically, checking and double-checking her recommendations and then taking out a stack of new material for Mary to type and carry back in a printout of the previous stack.

Sunday afternoon wore on as she sludged through the report. The noise in the outer office would stop periodically and Mary would come in to see if she wanted any coffee or sometimes urge her just to get up and walk down the hall to stretch her legs.

"Mary? It's nine thirty. Why don't you stop for the night?" Kay said, walking to the outer office. Her own tiredness was making her voice hoarse.

Mary hit the "file" key with obvious relief and sat back. "I'll start this printing so you can proof it first thing in the morning while I'm doing the rest of it." Her secretary eyed the sheaf of yellow paper in Kay's hand. "Is that the last of it?"

Giving her a weary smile, Kay nodded.

"I should be able to get it done by noon, then," Mary said.

"Great! And thanks, Mary," Kay said. "Southey may come out of this thing with a black eye, but we certainly won't." She only mouthed the encouraging words.

After her secretary had left, Kay sat in the quiet, empty building for an hour longer, staring off into space as she slowly rocked back and forth in her chair. Taking the phone, she dialed for a taxi. When the time came for its arrival, she stood up from her creaking chair, and walking in the darkened corridors to the glassed-in entrance, she'd never felt so alone in her life.

CHAPTER NINE

The report was finished, copied, and on Kay's desk by eleven the next morning. She eyed the two-inch stack of paper warily, wondering how such a benign-looking pile of words could have caused so much trouble and pain.

But she was proud of her company's work and it was with satisfaction that she called Gloria and Steve into her office to share the glory.

"So you did work on it in Big Bear!" Gloria said, with a look of surprise. "After you left, Mary told me it had been postponed by Southey. It took a lot of faith to keep working on it."

Kay lowered her eyes to the report. "I got word the project had been reactivated."

"Well, postponement or not, I would have been out on the lake, fishing all day!" Steve said with a laugh. But his lighthearted comment hit Kay too close to home and she stood up.

"I'll send it out this afternoon," she said.

"Send?" Gloria asked. "You mean you're not going to go over to Southey and plunk it down on Huntingdon's desk personally? You deserve to at least—"

"No!" Kay answered sharply. "No, I'm not. He'll need to read it anyway before he can comment on it, so it doesn't matter how it gets there, does it?"

Both of her employees wore puzzled looks as they left her office and she flush guiltily when the door shut behind them. She wanted to call them back and explain everything, but something made her refrain. She would tell them later.

The report was dutifully sent off. Mary silently brought in the signed delivery slip and placed it on Kay's desk. Burke's scrawled signature was at the bottom, staring out at her accusingly, calling her a coward.

Gloria offered her a ride home that night, but Kay accepted only as far as the garage where she'd had her car towed that morning. It was ready for her and she paid the astronomical bill without question, her mind absorbed with trying *not* to think about the president of Southey Manufacturing. The man behind the counter in greasy overalls must have anticipated an argument, for he shook his head in wonder.

Once at home she spent another difficult evening. But tonight it was too much for her, and ignoring the darkening overcast sky, she bounded out the front door wearing a patchwork pullover over an old pair of jeans. She hadn't even taken the time to put on socks under her running shoes.

She walked to a coffee shop six blocks away. Sitting in an isolated corner nursing a cup of Sanka, she realized her odd sensation of being removed from her surroundings wasn't going to go away as soon as she'd expected. It had taken up residence and she might as well get used to it.

It was nearing ten when the waitress came back to her table looking pointedly at her watch.

"Will there be anything else?"

Shaking her head no, Kay paid the bill and left. Waiting at the stoplight, she heard a car honk. A second later she heard her name being shouted and she instinctively turned to see who would be calling her. Three lanes away, in the left-turn lane, was Burke's Porsche, looking strangely purple under the mercury-vapor streetlight. He had started to get out when another car honked behind him; the left-turn arrow had appeared and he was holding up traffic. Shouting, "Wait!" to Kay, he slammed back into the car and squealed around the corner.

Panicking, she took off across the street as soon as the walk light blinked on. Burke had had to turn the wrong way but she didn't think it would take him long to catch up with her. She ran straight for her house, oblivious to everything but the image of her front door.

It had started to drizzle while she'd been in the coffee shop, but had stopped just as she'd left it. Now the rain returned harder than ever and she splashed through puddles, shaking her head to keep the water from running into her eyes.

It was an uphill trip and her legs ached, but she refused to stop as she ran from one circle of streetlamp light to the next. Her top was drenched and her jeans efficiently soaked up the water from the puddles, so she was drenched by the time she reached the corner near her home. In physical agony she walked the last few yards to her door, her breath coming in deep gulps and all her concentration focused on keeping her legs from buckling under her.

She stood staring at the steps, wondering how she was ever going to get up them, when a car pulled into the drive its headlights swinging over her. Knowing who it was without turning around, she just stood there, her head drooping and her shoulders slumped forward in resignation.

There wasn't any energy left to feel anger or fear or anything and when she heard a car door close she collapsed to a sitting position on the steps.

"Why did you come back?" she asked, her voice cracking with exhaustion. "I don't want to see you. I don't want to have anything to do with you." Her hair was hanging in streamers down her face and she pushed it back with no thought to her looks.

"Kay," he said, his own clothes darkening with the rain, "I just wanted to talk."

She was too tired to see the anguish in his face or hear the tremor in his voice above the pounding of the water on the driveway. "No, there's nothing to talk about."

"At least let's go in the house; we can't stay out here," he said.

"I'll go in, you go to your car. There's nothing to talk about!" Her words rose in pitch as her exhaustion and frustration edged toward hysteria.

"Kay, you'll make yourself ill if you stay out here much longer. I'll go and leave you alone, if that's what you want, but promise me you'll go inside."

Nodding, she propped herself up to a standing position. He came forward to help her, but she stumbled and fell against the door in her haste to get out of his way.

Without another word he turned and walked away.

Inside she managed to strip off her wet clothes before sitting down on the edge of her bed to dry herself.

Half an hour later she was coughing and an hour later she was curled up in the middle of her bed shivering under a mountain of blankets. She'd come down with a nasty cold.

By the time she was ready to go back to work, Gloria and Steve had taken over the Southey project completely. They'd talked with Burke and worked out a revised timeline and were hard at work on the design phase.

A month passed, during which time Kay didn't see or speak to Burke, having told Mary to refuse his frequent calls, but she knew the project was progressing ahead of schedule. He'd called her at home twice, but after she'd hung up on him the second time, he'd taken the hint.

She occupied herself with work, driving herself to write proposals for new contracts, overseeing the projects Gloria and Steve had been working on before taking on the Southey account. She was the busiest she'd ever been, but she was also the unhappiest.

In the past her work had always satisfied her; she could lose her anxiety in hard work and the intellectual stimulation it provided. But now it wasn't enough. And though she'd try one more proposal or one more long night's work on an existing contract, it still didn't erase the hollowness inside or free her from the rough-hewn face and blue eyes that could become almost black.

To her disgust she often caught herself thinking of what Burke might have said to her that rainy night. Grinding her teeth, she'd tell herself he would only have used plausible-sounding arguments to try to convince her of his innocence. But she knew better and she wasn't having any.

Her sister-in-law kept tabs on her, but had very little luck in getting her to slow down. Another month passed before she finally held out an inducement Kay couldn't turn down.

"It's Davy's birthday party! You've got to come next Sunday. You know he'd be crushed if his favorite aunt wasn't there."

"His only aunt!" Kay laughed. But she agreed to go and reminded Sally of the train set she'd hidden at Kay's.

Laughing, Sally said, "Do you know, I'd almost forgotten about that? That reminds me—how's Burke? Allen's been—"

"I have to go now, Sally. See you Sunday." The receiver clicked down on Sally's puzzled good-bye.

She swiveled back to her desk. The Southey project had started testing that morning and she was on edge. Late that afternoon she called Gloria and Steve into her office to see how things had gone.

"Great!" Steve said, grinning. "That Cath can sure write some fantastic video scripts! The students in the test training class were leaning forward in their seats to catch every word. How soon's she coming back? We need her!"

"Baby girls take a lot of time and energy!" Gloria interrupted. "And she's such a cute little thing."

"I bet she sleeps all the time—and Cath would go bonkers with nothing to do! She knows Pagel'll pay for day care, doesn't she?" Steve asked.

Kay quietly cleared her throat. "Cathy called me and said she's planning on coming back in two months. And yes, she knows about the day care." She wanted to get the conversation back on track. Happily married women with new babies was a subject she was curiously loath to discuss. "The Southey project?"

Gloria grinned at Steve, then at Kay. "As Steve said, it's going great. We still might run into some glitches, but so far everything's on target."

"Good. Keep me informed," she said in dismissal.

Going shopping for a birthday present for her nephew raised her low spirits considerably. And on an unexplained impulse she bought Cathy Miller's new baby a huge stuffed koala bear.

The following days passed quickly, with excellent reports coming in from the testing at Southey. Several times Kay almost gave in to the urge to go see it herself. In fact, for any other client, she would've been poring over the test results and comments, making sure nothing was missed. But in the end she convinced herself it was best to stay in the background.

On Friday Mary was sick and Kay was forced by her workload to call in temporary help. Fortunately the woman seemed capable and Kay relaxed as she went back to work.

She'd just hung up the phone and was wearing a wide smile—Pagel had been awarded a big contract with one of the large aerospace divisions based in San Diego—when her intercom buzzed.

"There's a call for you on line two, Dr. Pagel," the voice said.

"Thanks," she answered and picked up the receiver. "Kay Pagel."

"New secretary?" Burke's voice asked sardonically. "The old one always told me you were 'out.'"

"Burke!" Kay yelped. She was stunned; she'd forgotten

to tell the temporary secretary not to transfer his calls and now she was caught totally off guard.

"I see you remember my name, at least," he said. Though his voice had turned neutral, she thought she detected a note of amusement at her reaction.

"I need to see you on Monday," he said. He didn't wait for her denial, but went on, "The training will be done this afternoon and we need to go over the final plans for the implementation. Why don't we say nine?"

She licked her lips, staring at the phone's mouthpiece. His voice had renewed all the tremors she'd thought she'd been able to forget. She'd only thought of him twice yesterday—well, twice if one didn't count dreams—and she didn't.

Desperately wanting to say no, Kay closed her eyes and sighed, knowing it was her job to go see him, no matter what their personal relationship was. "Nine is okay with me," she said, her voice wavering slightly.

"Kay," he began.

"This is strictly business, Burke," she said before he could continue. "No more than that."

She fell silent, expecting him to respond. But he said nothing and she felt compelled to add, "Burke, you do understand that, don't you? We put ourselves in an impossible situation; it should never have happened, but it did. And now"—she faltered—"and now, there's nothing to do but put it behind us and go on with our lives. I have."

The minute she said it she knew it was a lie. She hadn't put him behind her; he would always be there, inside her heart.

But it sounded so final being put into words. Kay tried to convince herself it was what she wanted, what *had* to be done; she blinked several times to clear away the moisture that had gathered in her eyes and was unaware of the sigh that escaped her. A sigh that held all the unhappiness she'd felt since the day they'd left Big Bear.

"Kay, I've got a phone call to make," Burke said suddenly. "I'll talk with you later. Good-bye."

The buzzing of the dial tone told her he'd hung up, and she replaced the receiver, trying to ignore the emptiness she'd been so acutely reminded of.

The rest of the day dragged on; at every turn her mind's eye saw the last image she'd had of Burke—he was looking down at her as she sat on the steps watching his clothes darken with the rain.

She finally pulled into her driveway and walked wearily up those same steps. After changing into a jogging suit for comfort, she sat down in her living room and put her feet up. Why had she refused to listen to him that day? Because of what he'd almost done to Pagel Associates? She'd like to believe that, but she knew it wasn't the real reason.

It was a habit with her to get over pain quickly. As a child she'd always been the kind who ripped off a Band-Aid in one clean jerk, rather than endure the slow torment of peeling it back. The pain was more intense, but it lasted only a short while.

But this pain hadn't faded. She hadn't gotten over him; even in so short a while he'd become an integral part of her.

It was useless to think about him! Retrieving her briefcase from near the door, she threw herself into her work, then, near midnight, dropped into bed too exhausted to dream.

Saturday passed in a blur and Sunday dawned clear and bright as an exemplary San Diego day in early summer should. As she was trying to decide between dressing up or wearing something casual, Sally phoned to ask her to pick up some more ice cream on her way over. When Kay told her of her dilemma, Sally laughed.

"At a birthday party for a six-year-old? Casual, of course! That green velour short set of yours would be perfect."

Thanking her and promising to bring along the ice

cream, Kay hung up. The outfit Sally had mentioned was definitely comfortable and she quickly pulled on the pair of short dark-green running shorts and a V-necked sleeveless tank top.

Turning in front of the mirror, she noticed how the rich, plush look of the fabric accented her figure; and it did set off her hair nicely. She had let her hair fall in soft waves to her shoulders and she shook her head to feel the silken strands against her neck.

With a rueful laugh she reminded herself that it didn't matter how good she looked, she still wouldn't impress a bevy of six-year-olds if she didn't show up with the ice cream!

Stopping at the store for three half-gallons of chocolate chocolate chip, she drove up promptly at one o'clock, the screaming from the backyard telling her some of the guests had already arrived.

Sally greeted her with a hug, and adding Kay's presents to an enormous pile, led her out to the kitchen.

"Thanks for getting the ice cream. I don't know how I could have forgotten to get enough!" Sally said, busily mixing up the punch. "Allen's out on the porch playing with the kids, naturally. He's pitching for their softball game. Some of the other parents challenged the children to a game—I won't tell you who's losing!"

Laughing, Kay asked, "Is everybody here, then?"

Sally had been tasting the punch, but at Kay's question she hastily put down the cup and started digging around in the back of a cupboard.

"I hope I'm not short of glasses, too," she said, pulling out a stack of plastic ones. "Oh, no, a couple of people called and said they'd be a little late. Here, would you count these for me?"

Curious about Sally's topic jumping, but putting it down to the party, Kay counted the glasses and assured Sally there were enough. She walked out onto the patio and immediately wished she hadn't worn the outfit Sally'd suggested: several of the fathers were eyeing her.

It was one of the divorced fathers who sat down next to her when she went to sit on one of the lawn chairs scattered in the corner of the yard. He'd evidently elected to stay out of the game.

"Bobby tells me you're Davy's aunt," he said, pulling the light aluminum chair closer to hers. He smiled, which was more a matter of his lips receding from his teeth than any indication of amusement. Three months ago she might have considered him handsome, but now her eyes passed over his curly dark-brown hair. He was slender, but his chest wasn't broad and his hips were a bit too wide to be attractive. But sitting next to her with one leg casually draped over the other, he obviously expected her admiration. All she felt was impatience.

Kay forced herself to smile and nod at the accuracy of his statement. She knew she was mentally comparing him to Burke and the poor man was coming out badly. But as she opened her mouth to answer him more fully, another unattached father came up to sit at her other side.

"Lenny tells me you're Davy's aunt," the newcomer said. He was a similar, if slightly shorter, version of Bobby's father. The only difference between them as far as Kay could see was that the newcomer's hair was red and straight.

She tried very hard not to scream with impatience at these twits while they glared at and tried to frown one another away, but she almost lost her control when yet a third father walked up and stood slightly behind and to one side of Lenny's father. Grinning, he opened his mouth to say something, but Kay forestalled him.

"Yes, I'm Davy's aunt," she said with a false sweetness.

There was a commotion near the sliding glass doors indicating that one of the late-comers had arrived and Kay, a look of panic in her eyes, checked to see if yet another divorced father was being sent to harass her.

She stiffened when heard Sally cry, "Burke! I was so glad when you called and said you could make it after all!" He was standing under the awning, a can of soda in his hand. Kay met his eyes and their gaze held across the lawn while he set the drink down and walked over to her.

The miscellaneous fathers seemed to fade into the background as he came toward her, his tall, muscular grace at complete odds with the men around her.

He walked up to the front of her chair and stood there, his hands on his hips and a half-smile playing around his mouth.

"Hello, Kay."

"Hello, Burke."

He wore a light- and dark-green rugby shirt with a pair of close-fitting jeans, his blue eyes hidden by Carrere sunglasses. Kay suppressed a grin when she noticed that it was now the wives' turn to ogle one of Sally's guests.

Both Bobby's and Lenny's fathers were ill at ease, their chairs squeaking as they squirmed. Lenny's father stood up, and giving Burke a nervous glance, told Kay he thought it was his turn at bat. The other two fathers also found reasons to escape and he sat down next to her. He gave the impression of overpowering the fragile chair, though with his narrow hips he had no trouble sitting in it.

"Sally didn't tell me you'd been invited," she said, watching the grass curl around her bare toes after she'd kicked off her sandals.

"Would you have come if she had?" His resonant voice made her pulse beat a little faster.

"I wouldn't want to have missed Davy's birthday party," she said evasively, still not looking at him. Would she have come? She looked across the green grass at her nephew, who was intently watching the young girl at bat; then her eyes traveled back to Burke. Yes, she would have.

"I expected you at the testing. Pagel's work is impressive; it more than justifies the price you charge." It was disturbing not to be able to read his eyes behind the sunglasses, but she didn't think he was mocking her.

"Fortunately your opinion is shared by the Sonian Corporation," she told him with a touch of pride in her voice. "They awarded Pagel a major contract last Friday. That's why I was in such a good mood when you called."

"Congratulations. However, I hadn't realized you *were* in a good mood on Friday," he said, a smile softening his words.

She curled her toes, trying to grasp the individual blades. "Burke, what happened?" she asked softly.

She couldn't tell where he was looking, but his face was turned toward the gathering of children jumping up and down in excitement, their game apparently over.

"I don't really know. It seemed you had a personal demon to fight and when the Ticher thing blew up, the fight continued, but with Southey—and me—in the role of Mephistopheles. I tried to explain my position that rainy night, but you were rather adamant about my leaving. So I left."

Her gaze went back down to the grass.

"We were good together, Kay," Burke added quietly.

"It's over." Her heart lurched as she said it and her stomach started to tighten in response to the finality of the statement.

"I know."

Kay was adrift, her moorings cast aside. Clutching the arms of the chair, she had to look away so he couldn't see the anguish she knew was there. It was over. Somehow she hadn't ever quite believed it until he acknowledged it.

"Hey, you two! Come on!" Sally's voice called to them from the table under the awning. "Davy's going to open his presents now!"

Burke stood, holding out his hand to Kay, and she reluctantly accepted his assistance. The enveloping warmth spread up her arm, but they both went to the living room subdued. It was already crowded with the children and their parents and they slipped in at the back, the birthday boy seated in the center of a mass of presents, beaming at his parents.

Everyone quieted down and watched the small boy disappear beneath the mounds of wrapping paper, though his squeals of delight were enough to reassure everyone he was still there.

When he came to his aunt's presents, a set of dinosaur skeletons made out of wood, an inflatable tent, and a little carpet toy for his half-grown kittens, the pile of paper exploded as he jumped up and ran to Kay.

"Aunt Kay! Aunt Kay!" he said, charging through the mass of kids and parents to wrap his arms tightly around her legs. "It's perfeck! George and Casper'll like it gobs!" He craned his neck back and looked up into her face, a wide smile on his face.

Burke was leaning over watching Davy, and the little boy caught sight of him. "Hi, Mr. Hunt'don! Isn't this swell? I'm glad you're still Aunt Kay's boyfriend," Davy said as he scurried back to his pile of new treasures, leaving a blushing aunt behind.

The ice cream and cake were served in the backyard, the adults sitting under the awning and the children out in the grass. Burke sat next to Kay on the bench; it was almost the same position in which they'd sat together the last time they'd been there. She tried to keep a healthy few inches between them, but a libidinous wife on the other side of Burke kept crowding him in an effort to do exactly what Kay was trying to avoid.

Burke turned to her, licking excess ice cream off the corners of his mouth, reminding Kay of the morning in Big Bear when he licked away the butter dripping down her chin.

Laughing, Burke said, "You look like a little kid who's been denied a treat! Do you want some more cake?"

Feeling foolish at letting her emotions show so clearly, she nodded and held out her plate in an attempt to cover herself. The cake had been made in the shape of a clown and Burke sliced off a huge piece of orange hair and a blue ear.

He set it down in front of her with a grin and watched her. She hadn't wanted the cake in the first place and now she was going to have to eat this enormous piece!

"I can't eat all of that!"

"We can share it," he assured her.

Looking at him askance, she picked up her fork and cut off a small bite.

"You'll have to do better than that," he said, taking her fork from her and shearing off a big chunk of chocolate cake. "Here, this is more like it." He aimed the fork toward her and she had to open her mouth quickly or have it decorating the front of her top.

"Burke, this is silly." The huge piece filled her mouth and she felt her jaws would disconnect as she chewed it. With a sparkling glint in her eye she took the fork from him and cut off another big piece. But this time she reached over to scoop up a bite of ice cream as well and then carried it to Burke's mouth.

He didn't protest, as she had, but took the bite with with all the appearance of one who was used to being fed. At the last minute her hand had faltered, but he reached up and guided her the last few inches, parting his lips to accept the morsel.

Their game was unnerving but Kay didn't know how to stop it and it was with relief that she ate the last bite. Her pink tongue flicked out to gather in any crumbs she might have on her lips. Turning to Burke to make sure he wasn't getting any more cake, she discovered him looking intently at her lips and unconsciously licked them again in apprehension.

"You shouldn't do that in front of an ex-lover, Kay," he whispered to her, his words drowned out for everyone but her by the noise of the party. "It makes him remember just how much he's missing."

She quickly averted her eyes from his dark, stormy ones, but not soon enough to stop the sudden rushing of her blood. The thought that he had enjoyed their times together and that he actually missed her sent her heart into a fluttering dance, but she sternly reminded herself that he had nothing to lose by teasing her.

The others were rising, needing to move around after the refreshments, and she joined them. Going around cleaning up the paper plates and cups, she watched the others as they gravitated into one group or another. She saw Bobby's and Lenny's fathers off to one side, together with the other man who had walked up just as Burke had arrived. She shuddered, thinking she'd been lucky at least to avoid having to spend the entire afternoon being pursued by them. Why didn't they pick on some other poor unattached woman?

Then the realization hit that there *weren't* any other unattached women at the party! No, that wasn't quite true, she admitted as she looked around and spotted Sally's best friend with her latest "companion." And there were others, too, but they all had dates or friends of some sort with them. Curious. But she couldn't accuse *Sally* of such machinations! Surely it was just a coincidence that there was so little choice among the four unattached men at the party that she'd naturally chosen to stay with Burke. Still . . .

She absently tossed the trash into the giant garbage can and picked up what was left of the ice cream to put it back into the freezer. Burke was right behind her, though she didn't know it, and she was startled when the freezer door closed without her touching it.

Turning around, she discovered him hovering over her, his arm still on the refrigerator. He stood close to her, and alone with him in the room, she could smell his heady mixture of scents.

"I wanted to remind you of our appointment tomorrow. Nine o'clock sharp," he said, his breath on her brow accenting his words with a feather touch that made a tingle of pleasure wash over her face.

"I won't forget," she said, unaccountably breathless. He leaned closer, his head bent.

"Tomorrow you'll be all business again, and my sweet Kay will be hiding somewhere inside Dr. Pagel." His lips brushed her forehead. "I want a good-bye kiss. One to remember."

She swallowed hard and reminded herself to breathe. He was so close, and at that moment she wanted nothing more than to reach out and run her hand across the hard muscles of his chest. Did she dare? Licking her lips, she nodded.

Slowly his hands came down and gently pulled her to him, as if he were afraid that a sudden movement would make her shy away. Once held against that hard, unyielding surface, Kay pushed away all thoughts of tomorrow or yesterday and concentrated on the lips descending to hers *now*.

It was a kiss of a thousand kisses—his lips softly caressing hers again and again, breaking down her last wall of resistance like a battering ram of the finest velvet. His tongue teased the corner of her mouth and made tiny, devasting forays into her glistening inner lips.

Her teeth parted in a welcoming sigh that their hearts heard, if not their ears. It was a kiss that made her feel at once at home and far away discovering new exotic places her mind had not even conceived.

No part of her was left untouched by the incandescence that flared to life deep within her. Her arms had found their way around his neck and her hands wandered over his back in glorious indulgence. But her fingers, playing an instinctive rhythm of slight pressure, felt his muscles stiffen as he prepared to end the kiss and she knew a moment of supreme sadness. All the world he had revealed to her was being withdrawn.

The blond head drew away and she watched him with

eyes the color of the darkest topaz, full of an uneasy mixture of anguish and desire.

"Burke," she whispered, but he shook his head and put a silencing finger on her lips.

His voice so low she could hardly hear him, he said, "Tomorrow." He gave her one last feather kiss and left.

The kiss had been more than a good-bye kiss for Kay; it had been an introduction. The dull ache that had lodged near her heart had gone the minute he'd sat down next to her in the lawn chair. And now she recognized the ache—it was an ache of incompleteness.

It had only been after she'd met him that she'd discovered she wasn't whole, that there was a part of her missing; and though she'd waited so patiently for the ache to go away, she knew now that it would be with her forever.

She slumped against the refrigerator at the thought. As trite as the saying was, forever *was* a long time. Too long to go through life haunted by the memory of Burke Huntingdon. Or at least haunted by too *short* a memory of Burke Huntingdon. Their lives might be so divergent as to be unable to mesh permanently, but why give up the time they did have? Or was it too late?

Smiling at her burgeoning idea, she straightened herself, pulling her shoulders back and inhaling deeply. "Tomorrow," he'd said. Tomorrow would be her last chance; after that Pagel Associates would no longer be involved with Southey Manufacturing. But if she had anything to say about it, Pagel's president would be *very* involved with Southey's!

She marched out to join the party in the backyard, still in full swing. Noticing Burke had left, she shrugged, telling herself his absence only gave her more time to gather her wits about her. She snatched up her startled nephew and planted a wet, smacking kiss on his cheek before joining the group in a rowdy game of tag. Tomorrow!

CHAPTER TEN

The next morning she was wide awake the instant she opened her eyes. It was earlier than she normally awoke but, with a smile hovering around her lips, she got up and ran a tub of hot water. She used plenty of bath crystals scented with her favorite perfume, and the entire room was soon filled with a lovely cloud of it.

She luxuriated in the mounds of suds and exotic perfume. When she had finished, she dusted on a light film of power with the same scent and dabbed the precious amber fluid of the perfume itself on all her pulse spots and anywhere else heat might gather to dissipate the intoxicating fragrance.

Walking to her bureau with the same secret smile, she purposely chose the most devastating underthings she owned. A bra that was really only two tiny strips of satin and lace, and panties that weren't much more. She reached for a pair of her regular pantyhose, then put them back in the drawer and searched for the pair of silk stockings she'd been saving for a special occasion. If she didn't think this day was special—no day would be.

Wearing the lacy garter belt that the stockings required had an added benefit. It made her feel sexy and just a touch decadent, two feelings she was going to need for her appointment this morning. Those, and every ounce of courage she could gather.

The pièce de résistance was a devastating raw-silk suit in a deep, rich brown that emphasized the gold in her hair and her eyes and the luster of her tanned skin. A cream-colored blouse of shimmering finished silk was added and she slipped into a pair of high-heeled brown leather shoes that drew attention to her slender ankles.

Quickly sweeping her hair up into a sophisticated topknot, she let a few strands purposely escape the pins and fall in soft tendrils to frame her face. She was especially careful with her makeup, being sure to use the contouring color to point up her high cheekbones and the smoky topaz of her eyes.

Finally she stepped back into her bedroom and examined herself closely in the mirror. The image there was unrecognizable. No, on second thought, Kay Pagel was beneath the sophisticated—and definitely sexy—woman staring out at her. And that Kay Pagel was smiling.

The suit skirt clung to her small waist and the feminine curves of her hips as if magnetized. The skirt was deeply slashed up the front, giving, with each step, a provocative glimpse of her long, shapely golden legs.

The blouse was the most expensive one she owned and its fit was worth every penny. The high collar was gently ruffled around the top, adding the only frivolous touch to the entire ensemble, making its flirting impact doubly effective. But most arresting of all was the deceptively demure neckline. At first glance it seemed closed all the way up. But in reality the blouse was unfastened for half its length, the deep décolletage opening a tiny bit with every movement she made, revealing the gentle swell of her breasts.

Heads turned to admire her when she walked into Pagel Associates that morning. Her employees' eyes were wide with surprise as as they watched her stride down the hallway to her office with a confident swing to her hips.

Mary, pausing only to glance up from her work, said, "I got your note; everything's ready and sitting on your desk...." Her voice trailed off as she finally took a good look at her boss.

Kay smiled her thanks and walked through the door to her office, leaving a secretary capable of whispering no more than a stunned "Wow!"

The next half-hour was spent making doubly sure everything was in order for the final presentation to Southey. All of Gloria's and Steve's notes on implementation were there as well as representative training materials. Everything was ready.

At ten to nine she drove into Southey's parking lot. She went through the lobby to the bank of elevators, oblivious to the people crowding the place. The doors of the elevator gasped open on the top floor. The quiet, plush atmosphere of the executive floor was at odds with her excitement, but she ignored it. She ignored everything but the wide oak doors at the end of the hallway and the desk that stood guard.

She started walking toward those doors, reminding herself to calm down—she was going to need every ounce of her usual calm control to pull off the daring bid she had planned. Her brow furrowed in a frown, though, as she walked closer and could not see anyone seated outside Burke's office. Surely someone was there to announce her? It would not suit her at all to have to knock and enter meekly at his command!

As she got closer, however, a patch of blue bobbed just beyond the wooden desktop, and she saw a plump, middle-aged woman digging at a lower drawer with a letter opener.

The woman sat up and saw Kay. "Oh! I didn't know anyone was there. This dratted desk is locked up tighter than a drum and I can't get it open. Carol Walsh probably took the keys with her out of spite!"

"I have an appointment to see Bur—Mr. Huntingdon at nine o'clock," Kay said, looking at the wall clock and seeing the hand a minute away from nine.

"Let's see...." The older woman searched the cluttered desktop for an appointment book. "Here it is! Ummm, you must be Dr. Pagel." Kay nodded once. "I'll tell Mr. Huntingdon you're here." She spoke into the intercom. "There's a Dr. Pagel here to see you, Mr. Huntingdon. She has an appointment."

His voice, strong and deep, replied, "Send her in, Mrs. Everest."

The secretary smiled and nodded Kay to the door. "Go on in, dear."

Kay faced the ceiling-high door and felt a tingling ribbon of fear snake down her back. A movement in the corner of her eye caught her attention—it was her reflection in the glass of a nearby picture. She saw the tall, sophisticated woman look back at her and it gave her confidence to continue with the game she'd started. Her feet began moving of their own volition, and in the space of a heartbeat she discovered her hand on the doorknob and her wrist turning. Without another pause she entered the familiar room.

He sat behind his massive desk, remote and completely unlike the man he'd been yesterday. But his eyes widened as he watched her cross the room, traveling down to her elegantly clad feet and back up to her face, hesitating for long moments on the tantalizing length of leg her skirt revealed as well as the teasing glimpses of golden skin exposed by her blouse when she walked.

His breath seemed to quicken as she neared his desk and stood in front of him. She did not sit down at first, but relished towering over him, if only for a short time.

"I trust you've brought the final report," he said, his voice rougher than it had been over the intercom.

The briefcase came up and was laid on his desk. She opened it with deliberate slowness, feeling that the intangible balance of power in the room had somehow tilted to her side for the moment and planning on using it to her full advantage. Placing a neat binder filled to capacity in front of him, she smiled and said, "Pagel's report." She was pleased at the hint of sardonic challenge in her voice and her smile widened as the golden fire in her eyes dared him to discover a flaw.

A spark of admiration flashed through his eyes and his head lowered in a barely perceptible nod as he acknowledged a worthy opponent.

"Have a seat, Kay," he said. The main event was about to begin.

She closed the case but left it on his desk. By sitting down she lost some of the advantage she'd had standing. To recover it she sat back in the chair, crossing her legs and letting the slash in her skirt fall open well above her knees. Deliberately waiting until his eyes returned to her face, she said, "Thank you."

As he quickly flipped through the dividers, she began noticing odd details, such as how his hand-tailored suit fit him so disturbingly well and how the white shirt underneath pulled ever so slightly across his broad chest.

With an elegant wave of her hand she dismissed such troublesome thoughts for the moment and indicated the report.

"You already know the basics," she said. "Most of the details are listed in the primary report in front, with the supplementary reports dealing with each individual aspect of the training program. They're filed in the latter part of the binder."

He nodded and continued to read a paragraph or two in each section before turning to the next. His finger tapped a particular place on a page and he said, "We've been working with Dolran Electronics on this part about adding an adjustable 'pause' cycle to the machines to allow for individual differences. I've been very impressed with their work."

"Dolran! That's the company Allen works for!" She leaned forward in surprise, completely unaware of the extraordinarily desirable picture she made. Her blouse had fallen open to reveal the swell of her breasts, rising and falling as she breathed. His eyes flashed again and this time they darkened with more than admiration.

He leaned forward as well, his shirt straining across his chest, and her tongue licked her lower lip in an unconscious gesture to combat the stirrings she was feeling just by being in his presence. What was happening to her plan?

"I've been working with Allen for the past month and a half. Didn't you know?"

"Oh! No, no, I didn't," she stuttered. This was not at all the way she'd planned for things to go! He was supposed to find her irresistible and yet here they were, a large oak desk still between them. What could she do to salvage the situation? She was starting to panic, but in a flash of recall she remembered his tactics in Big Bear and instantly decided to turn the tables on him and see what happened. After all, how else could he smell her perfume?

"Why don't you read the report more thoroughly?" she said, her voice lower than before.

He looked up at her for a moment, then asked, "Do you want me to read it now? It *would* be easier to ask you questions instead of making notes, but can you spare the time?"

Could she spare the time when her whole future happiness was at stake? Damn right! But all she answered was "Of course, Burke. Pagel Associates believes in giving full service to its client companies." The seductive note in her voice made a dark-blond eyebrow rise in speculation and she quickly pushed away professional qualms at using the client-contractor relationship to further her personal ends. But it had to be done! She settled deeper in her chair, unobtrusively hitching up the skirt a bit higher so he could get a healthy view of her golden thigh.

His eyes never leaving her, he reached over to the intercom and spoke to the new secretary. "Mrs. Everest? Please get us a fresh pot of coffee and cancel the rest of my appointments for today."

"All of them, Mr. Huntingdon?" asked the startled woman.

"All of them, Mrs. Everest."

"Yes, sir."

Burke sat back in his leather chair, apparently postponing reading the report until the coffee had arrived. To fill the silence between them, Kay asked curiously, "What happened to Miss Walsh? She seemed efficient, if not very friendly."

Burke chuckled. "So, you're finally curious about that, are you? I've tried to tell you twice now, but you would have none of it."

The coffee arrived before his could expand on that intriguing statement, and he rose and wheeled the cart into the room, politely dismissing Mrs. Everest with a thank-you and a nod. Pouring her a cup of coffee, she watched him put in just the right amount of sugar and cream before handing it to her.

She started to take a sip and almost choked on the scalding liquid as, after he'd poured himself a cup, he walked over to the chair next to hers and sat down instead of sitting back behind his desk. It was what she'd wanted, but it had been much easier to think when the massive oak desk had been between them.

"So, you want to know what happened to Miss Walsh," he said, settling in the chair so he was leaning slightly toward her. His eyes rested briefly on the enticing V-shaped portion of skin the blouse opened to his view. He took a sip of coffee before resuming.

"Both Ticher and Carol Walsh had been employed by George Southey, and when he'd sold the company, he'd asked ESSCO to keep them on and we'd agreed."

"Miss Walsh was with Ticher?" Kay asked, her interest in his explanation overcoming her fear of his closeness. She set her cup down on the edge of his desk and turned toward him, the better to give him her full attention. As she did so, her skirt, without her knowledge this time, hiked up even farther. "I admit I didn't expect that."

"Things often happen that we don't expect," he said, the slight waver in his voice making him clear his throat before he continued. "The problem was really one of misguided loyalty. Even though George had assured them he was selling the company because he'd wanted to, and not because we'd done some grand wheeling and dealing for stock, they didn't believe him and set out to . . . make things difficult for the new owners of Southey."

Now that her personal antagonism for this man had vanished, she found herself really interested in discovering what had actually happened. She must have instinctively known he couldn't have been such a villain in the piece but had had to block out all valid explanations to keep her own involvement at a minimum.

Her full attention on him, she leaned forward slightly to rest her chin on her hand, her elbow supported by the arm of the chair, thus incidentally revealing an even more tantalizing view of her décolletage. Without knowing it, she was being devastatingly successful in her plan.

"So where did Pagel fit into all of this?" she asked.

He took a deep breath and briefly closed his eyes. It was almost as if he were savoring some delicious smell, but Kay, her mind on his explanation, decided he was only trying to order his thoughts.

"To be honest, that was a miscalculation on our part. We knew someone in the company had nothing but antipathy for the new owners, but not who. When he argued so vociferously for a postponement of Pagel's project—yes, it was he—we started to get suspicious, but still had no proof."

"But right after the project had been postponed, you went off to Big Bear with me!" Kay said. "How could you afford to be away?"

To her surprise he gave a shout of laughter and grinned

at her like a mischievous little boy. "*That* was the biggest stroke of luck in my entire life!"

"Luck?"

His blue eyes gazed into hers, their smoky depths revealing an emotion she couldn't read. "Luck," he said with such heartfelt conviction that Kay knew there was a great deal unsaid.

"When I got back to the office after having had lunch with you," he said, dropping his eyes from hers, "Robert Scarp called me and said he felt the best way to catch the 'problem factors,' as he called them, was to give them enough rope.

"To do that he suggested I go away for a week, only calling in now and again to keep up appearances. So when I drove to your place to apologize, I could hardly believe my luck when I found you leaving." He raised his eyes once more to hers, and their dark swirling currents proclaiming his sincerity, he said, "I'd never believed in fate before, but that day I discovered it with a capital *F!*"

Their eyes held once more, neither one of them capable, for several seconds, of breaking the contact. Burke was the one who finally looked away, standing quickly and refilling his cup. He didn't resume his seat beside her, but went back to sit behind his desk.

Waving an impatient hand, he said, "The rest you've probably figured out. Ticher and Carol Walsh picked Pagel Associates as a target in order to wreck the equilibrium of Southey's new owners—which they did more successfully than they'll ever know." The last was said so bitterly that Kay opened her mouth to ask what he meant, then closed it, not sure she wanted to hear the answer just yet.

"Now that that's out of the way, let's get back to this report," he said gruffly, immediately picking up the notebook Kay had given him and turning to a section near the front.

He bent over the report and Kay studied him closely.

A lock of blond hair had fallen onto his forehead and his hand absently kept trying to brush it back. She noted every line of his face, the strength of his jaw that was offset by the thin, sensual mouth that her own lips remembered so well.

He looked up at that moment, catching a tender smile on her face, and his words were spoken in a vague sort of way, as if what he was saying had nothing to do with what he was thinking.

"This passage keeps referring to SMEs. I'm not that familiar with all the terms used in your profession. What does it mean?" he asked. "I remember Steve used it once, too."

She started to answer him, but the look in his eyes jarred her plan back into her mind. Maybe she was making more progress than she'd realized. Taking advantage of it, she rose and filled her coffee cup before answering him. Walking around the end of his desk, she took a sip of coffee and set it down out of her way and casually perched on the edge of his desk, her crossed knees very close to the hand he was resting on the arm of his chair. She felt like some brazen secretary and smiled at the idea—at that moment she and a brazen secretary had a lot in common!

Leaning back on one hand, she said, "SME stands for subject-matter expert. In this case our subject-matter experts were those people who really knew how to run the machines—as well as they could be run under the difficult conditions. And Mr. Johnson, of course," she added with an impish grin.

He merely grunted and frowned at her, and bent back over the report. Kay grinned to herself. Maybe her plan was working! His manner of ignoring her presence was too studied to be real.

She hopped down, afraid of being too obvious. Leaning over his shoulder, she put a casual hand on his back as she pointed out a particular feature of what he was reading. "This is where Johnson's report was invaluable."

He made a vague affirmative noise deep in his throat and Kay decided to back off to give him some breathing room. Trailing her hand across his back as if nonchalantly withdrawing it, she picked up her coffee and went to stand by the smoked-glass window. She didn't even see the colorful scene below as she pondered her problem.

Wasn't he being just a little too stoic? Perhaps she had misinterpreted his kiss yesterday—maybe it *had* been a farewell kiss. Ending their brief affair as he probably had dozens of others. She could barely swallow the rest of her coffee.

Setting the empty cup on the tray, she told herself not to be a fool. Giving up too soon only turned a possible defeat into a definite one.

At noon Mrs. Everest brought in a tray of sandwiches and promptly withdrew after giving Kay a sidelong glance.

Kay put a sandwich near Burke's hand and went back to sit in the chair she'd occupied earlier. Occasionally he would ask her a question, and she would hover close enough to him allow him to smell her perfume; but she didn't touch him again.

He asked her questions often enough to prevent her from starting to work on anything else. That left her with plenty of time to think—and most of her thoughts centered around the man sitting hunched over the brown binder.

Several more hours passed and Kay started to weary of her game. Biting her lip in disappointment, she was ready to give up and admit defeat. But some last shred of hope convinced her to stay until he'd finished reading through the hefty report. He evidently planned on reading every single word in the entire binder.

Finally he closed the notebook and sat watching her as she closed the blinds to the bright rays of the late-afternoon sun.

Clearing his throat again, he said, "I have some things I'd like to discuss."

Three more hours passed, but this time Kay wasn't aware of it. She was deep into a discussion of how the implementation of their training project would take place. When she had finished, she sat back, tired but satisfied with her own and her company's work. The fading orange glow seeping through the blinds told her the sun was finally setting.

"I accept the Pagel project as it is represented here and based on what I've seen in testing," he said, his voice oddly strained. "You can send us the final bill; the project is over." With deliberate slowness he picked up the binder and stood. Not understanding what he was doing, Kay stood also, her heart in her throat at her obvious failure.

Not quite knowing what to do, she saw Burke turn and put the binder on the credenza behind him. Unwilling to swallow the bitter pill of failure just yet, she turned and walked to the windows, reopening the blinds one by one to the San Diego evening. As the light dimmed, she could see the streetlights coming on, the pale pink glow flickering at her feet.

She turned back to Burke's desk. He was standing to one side of it, watching her. She returned his look with her longing for him in her eyes.

He closed the gap between them in three long strides, pulling her to him and kissing her with a passion that suspended time. She could think of nothing, feel nothing, but his lips on hers, their mouths blending into a complete extension of their desire.

Their tongues caressed with a thoroughness of renewing cherished memories. They had been away from each other too long, the kiss of the day before only serving to arouse passions they had forced beneath the surface.

His hands roamed over her body, reaching inside her jacket to run along her silk-clad back. Her own hands were reaching inside the collar of his jacket to feel the taut muscles just below the surface of his skin.

He lifted his head and they were both breathing in gasps of air.

"God, how I've wanted to do that," he said as his hand began to unbutton her blouse. "I want you, Kay. I want you now and I want you always! This thing has almost destroyed my control too many times today—it goes!"

"Burke, what are you talking about? You've been sitting there like a lump all day! How can you say you want me?" The intense fire in his eyes answered her and she stepped back from his embrace. Her blouse was unbuttoned but her hands stayed at her sides.

Looking out at the sparkling lights of the city, she said quietly, "And how can you talk of always? No matter how much I want you, need you"—she buried her face in her hands, then looked up at him—"no matter how much I *love* you, I know there can never be an 'always' with us. One day ESSCO will take over another company and need you to put it in order. And I couldn't go with you."

He ran a tender hand along her jaw. "My sweet Kay." Glancing up at the ceiling lights, he quickly strode over to the switch and turned them off, then moved to lock the door. In the darkness lit only by the lights from the city filtering through the smoked glass, he walked back to her and gathered her into his arms.

"There *can* be an 'always' with us, Kay. I've been—"

"Burke," she interrupted, "remember that morning I ran out of the house in Big Bear?" When he nodded, she went on, talking into the soft material of his shirt. "I was hurt and confused about our relationship. I knew I should never have let it go so far, and yet I couldn't help myself. Something about you kept drawing me back as if the passions you aroused in me were so elemental they were beyond my control."

He tightened his hold on her briefly to express his agreement.

"I was scared to death," she said, almost inaudibly. "The night before, I would have given up everything, my work, my company, my family, *everything* for you. I couldn't face those kinds of feelings—so I ran."

A tear fell down her cheek, but she didn't care as she looked up into the face of the one man she loved and would always love. That was one "always" that would be with her.

"But I can't bear the hollowness I've felt these past two months. I want to be with you, Burke, for as long or as short a time as we have."

He kissed her tenderly, his lips warm and caressing.

"It will be as long as always, Kay. ESSCO offered me the permanent position as Southey's president and I accepted."

He tilted her chin up to bring her face close to his. Covering her face with tiny kisses that sent darts of desire to the center of her being, he said, "And now, Dr. Kay Pagel, would you be willing to marry a lowly mister? Two corporate presidents in a family *always* make things more interesting, don't you think?"

Kay smiled a slow, sensuous smile that quickened the throbbing beat at Burke's throat. "I don't know, Burke. Executive decisions require a great deal of supporting information. Such as what happens when I do this. . . ." She loosened his tie and started to unbutton his shirt, running her fingertips under the fabric and making light traces with her fingernails.

"Or this . . ." She finished unbuttoning the shirt and ran her hand over his flesh, feeling the hard muscles of his back respond to the touch of her fingertips. "Or this . . ." she said, her voice low with her mounting passion as her hand unbuckled his belt and undid the tiny button at the waistband of his pants and then slid down and around his waist, running just inside the elastic band of his shorts.

His arms tightened, crushing her to his body. His voice came from deep within his chest. "Or this," he said.

The driving force of his lips parted her own in willing compliance and their mouths were joined as one. Her tongue explored his warmth, the territory now familiar and special, and his tongue ran lightly over the moist smoothness before tasting the edges of her questing tongue.

All her senses turned inward to absorb the feeling of his hands traveling over her body under the silk blouse. He caressed the slick satin of her bra, and she could feel the nipples beneath his hand grow and strain against the soft material in exquisite agony.

Drawing his hand across her back with a slowness that belied his passion, he undid the catch to her bra. He held her breasts' fullness, his thumb and index finger gently pulling and rolling the taut nipple in an excruciating rhythm. The ball of spinning celestial fire was gathering at the core of her womanhood, its urge for release expanding and strengthening with each foray of his tongue and each pass his thumb made over the dark tip of her breast.

Her lips were on his neck, taking tiny nips in the sensitive flesh just under and behind his ear. He trailed kisses along her neck and shoulders, his tongue sending shimmering heat through her while her own tongue teased the convoluted paths in his ear.

Then his head lowered and his teeth captured an erect nipple. She gasped in sensuous delight when he carefully nibbled the very tip, the blood roiling through her veins with a primal fire.

He raised his head, eliciting a groan from Kay as he left off his glorious feast. His hands reached inside her jacket, and with a long caress down her arms, took it off and tossed it onto the floor a few feet away. Her hands repeated the long, sensuous stroke down the muscled undulations of his arms and soon his jacket was also on the floor. Her blouse and bra were quickly followed by his shirt onto the growing pile of discarded clothes.

He embraced her, one hand reveling in the satin feel of

her bare back and the other struggling with the fastener of her skirt. Her inquisitive fingers had already unfastened the waistband of his pants, and after her skirt had slid to the floor and been kicked aside, she slowly drew the zipper down. She could feel his desire for her as she leaned over and took nipping kisses low along his stomach while her hands pulled his pants lower and lower till they fell to the floor. His shorts soon followed.

Standing upright, she took a step back from him and let her eyes wander over his naked form. She wanted to cool off just a bit, remembering the ecstatic heights his slow, sensual lovemaking had taken her to their last night in Big Bear.

She watched his chest expand and contract in deep breaths. "I hope you know what you're doing to me, standing there in that garter belt and those stockings." He closed the space between them and held her close; then the rest of her clothes were quickly discarded. His lips tasted her hair while he whispered, "God, how I need you!"

He drew her down to the floor with him and they lay on their sides, his mouth on hers in a deep binding kiss. "My sweet Kay, how I love you. . . ." he whispered.

Kay rolled onto her back, one breast cupped by his hand as he teased the nipple to attention once again. His other hand felt the curve of her waist and hips, traveling to her thighs, which parted naturally to let his hand explore the soft inner flesh.

His hand cupped her womanhood and her body arched in response. He was kissing her now along a fiery trail across her flat stomach down to the edge of his hand. Her hips rose to his touch and his fingers gently sank into her velvet softness. Circles of radiating heat poured out, filling her with a liquid warmth.

Her entire consciousness was focused on the pleasure emanating from Burke's touch. He took her higher and higher, until she cried out for him to come to her and release the exquisite tenseness. With a slight movement he was above her, his lips kissing her eyes, forehead, and lips. She could feel the furnacelike heat from his desire resting against her thigh for a brief moment until, leaving a burning path, he approached the molten source of her passion.

She cried out her joy at the moment of their joining, her mind and heart fused together by the feeling of completeness that enveloped her. Moving in the elemental rhythm of their love, Kay lost coherent thought as the blood pounding through her pulsed to their rhythm.

Her hands roamed over the expanse of his back, her fingertips craving the heat of his skin. As she came closer and closer to being overwhelmed by the intensity of her release, her hands ventured lower to grasp his tight round buttocks, pulling him to her.

The startled gasp forced from Burke was immediately followed by a groan wrenched from deep within him. Kay's own mindless cry of pleasure joined with his as they reached the very limits to which their bodies could take them.

Kay lay snuggled next to Burke and he softly kissed her temple, his breath warm against her skin.

"I want us to be married as soon as we can," he told her, his eyes watching his hand run down the valley between her breasts to her stomach. "Can you move in tonight?"

She chuckled softly, a tender smile playing around her lips. "I don't think we can be married *that* soon!"

Nuzzling behind her ear, he said, "These past two months have been hell without you. And today! I thought I'd go mad! You don't know what you do to a man." He broke off his kisses and brought his head up to look at her as she giggled.

"You *do* know! That suit wasn't fair; when you walked in, it was all I could to to keep from pulling you into my lap and ravishing you!"

"It was about as fair as your 'last kiss' yesterday. As if I could walk away from that!"

Smiling, he said, "Liked it, did you?"

An answering smile deep in her eyes, she murmured her assent and reached up to draw his lips down to hers.

She felt him responding, and she broke away for a moment. "Burke—are you sure? Marriage is a major commitment; wouldn't you rather just live together for a while and see if we're compatible?"

"I thought we were pretty compatible in Big Bear, honey," he said, kissing her bottom lip. "And I plan on tying us together in every way—spiritual and temporal—I can find!" He kissed her fiercely, his hand running down the peaks and valleys of her body.

"Love's the commitment, honey," he told her when the kiss ended. "Marriage just makes the loving easier."

She leaned into him, her arms wrapping around his neck and her eyelids heavy with desire. "In that case," she said, "let's have some more of that easy lovin'."

LOOK FOR NEXT MONTH'S
CANDLELIGHT ECSTASY ROMANCES ®

170 PROMISES IN THE NIGHT, *Jackie Black*
171 HOLD LOVE TIGHTLY, *Megan Lane*
172 ENDURING LOVE, *Tate McKenna*
173 RESTLESS WIND, *Margaret Dobson*
174 TEMPESTUOUS CHALLENGE, *Eleanor Woods*
175 TENDER TORMENT, *Harper McBride*
176 PASSIONATE DECEIVER, *Barbara Andrews*
177 QUIET WALKS THE TIGER, *Heather Graham*

When You Want A Little More Than Romance—

Try A Candlelight Ecstasy!

Dell — **Wherever paperback books are sold!**

NEW DELL

Candlelight Ecstasy Supreme

TEMPESTUOUS EDEN,
by Heather Graham.
$2.50

Blair Morgan—daughter of a powerful man, widow of a famous senator—sacrifices a world of wealth to work among the needy in the Central American jungle and meets Craig Taylor, a man she can deny nothing.

EMERALD FIRE,
by Barbara Andrews
$2.50

She was stranded on a deserted island with a handsome millionaire—what more could Kelly want? Love.

Desert Hostage

Diane Dunaway

Behind her is England and her first innocent encounter with love. Before her is a mysterious land of forbidding majesty. Kidnapped, swept across the deserts of Araby, Juliette Barclay sees her past vanish in the endless, shifting sands. Desperate and defiant, she seeks escape only to find harrowing danger, to discover her one hope in the arms of her captor, the Shiek of El Abadan. Fearless and proud, he alone can tame her. She alone can possess his soul. Between them lies the secret that will bind her to him forever, a woman possessed, a slave of love.

A DELL BOOK   11963-4 $3.95

At your local bookstore or use this handy coupon for ordering:

Dell DELL BOOKS   DESERT HOSTAGE   11963-4 $3.95
P.O. BOX 1000, PINE BROOK, N.J. 07058-1000

Please send me the above title. I am enclosing $ _____ (please add 75c per copy to cover postage and handling. Send check or money order—no cash or C.O.D.'s. Please allow up to 8 weeks for shipment.

Name _____

Address _____

City _____ State/Zip _____